One

Good

Turn

One Good Turn

By
Sarah Wallace

Book Two in Meddle & Mend

For those who are searching for where they belong:
this book is for you.

CONTENTS

CONTENT WARNINGS

One Good Turn takes place in the same world as *Letters to Half Moon Street* but explores the underbelly of London. As such there are some darker elements in this story. My books will always be about the power of kindness and hope and will always end happily, but please note that this book includes the following:

- economic hardship
- a side character in an abusive relationship (including grooming and sex trafficking)
- characters who have chosen sex work

CHAPTER 1

THE DAY that ultimately changed Nell Birks's life started as a rather ordinary one.

She had gone to work at Smelting's Spell Shop, one of her various odd-jobs. Of all of these odd-jobs, Nell liked working at Smelting's best of all. Though the work was less creative and more mundane than many of the other jobs she did, and Smelting—mean old crank that he was—paid her poorly, it was a good sight better than being a thief and forever looking over her shoulder.

On a chilly day between winter and spring, Nell was sweeping the shop briskly while Mr. Smelting worked in the back room. Her task was disrupted by a toff who strode into the store and looked about as if he were a little lost. He was tall with broad, muscled shoulders. He had large, dark, angular eyes, a wide nose, strong jaw, and wide mouth. His skin was tan in color, but Nell was sure it was not the result of too many hours in the sun; he was far too finely dressed to be the type who worked outdoors, and too finely dressed to be mucking about in her corner of London, for that matter. She recognized the elegant stitching of his coat, the curl of his hat brim, and the crispness of his cravat for what they were: quality.

She groaned inwardly. She'd seen gents of his ilk before, although admittedly they weren't usually shopping for spells. Usually, they were looking for some cheap pleasure or to hawk some family heirloom to pay off creditors.

So she was surprised when the gentleman smiled at her and said, "Good morning, friend. I'm looking to buy some ingredients, but unfortunately, I have little understanding of these things." This was said with a self-deprecating smile. "I would be very grateful if you could assist."

Nell was taken aback by how readily the gentleman accepted her as a source of knowledge. She couldn't decide if his mistake made him seem foolish or kind.

She shook her head. "I'd better fetch Smelting for you."

His grin broadened. "Much obliged."

As promised, she fetched Smelting, a short and scrawny older man with leathery skin. As soon as the spellmaster was out of the backroom, Nell did what she normally did and pocketed a few discarded items. She enjoyed being surrounded by magic work. She had never admitted this fascination with anyone else; they would have scoffed at her for wanting something so above her own station.

Nell had crafted her own education from observing Smelting's work and the street magicians who did the flashy sort of spells that people paid money to see. She had mastered a few spells: one that temporarily made things weightless, a persuasion spell, and her favorite—a look-away spell. She was most proud of the last one, because she had worked it out on her own. She had seen a street magician performing a spell to turn things invisible and tried to mimic it. Though she had never successfully turned anything invisible, in attempting to teach herself the invisibility spell, she had discovered that twisting her wrist in a certain way could sometimes cast a spell that made people not *quite* notice her.

She tucked a small sprig of rosemary in her left pocket (good for both the persuasion spell and the look-away spell).

When she found a slightly crumpled feather in the corner of the room, still fluffy enough to be useful for the spell that made things weightless, she stowed it safely in her shirt pocket. Smelting always let things go to waste.

She strode through the backroom swiftly, keeping an ear to the conversation in the shop. The gentleman shopper didn't seem to know very much about magic.

"And what spell is this item used for?" he asked Smelting. "Is it dangerous? Does it need to be treated? This looks interesting. What is it? Is it useful? Do you have any ingredients that might be harder for a spellcaster to acquire? This is quite a pretty flower. Is it—oh, what a shame."

She wondered why he had bothered to come all this way if he was so inexperienced.

She came out of the backroom and returned to her sweeping, trying not to be obvious in her eavesdropping. She had a bad feeling about the gentleman coming into the shop. Not only did people of his station rarely meander to the neighborhood, they rarely still made it out with their purses. Sometimes they never made it out at all. The ones who made a practice of coming to the brothels knew to at least cover themselves with shabby cloaks to appear slightly less conspicuous. But this bloke carried his wealth easily on his shoulders. She was frankly surprised he had survived to the shop in the first place.

Nell ducked outside to see if the customer had attracted any hopeful stragglers. Sure enough, her best friend Philip Standish was hovering near the door with Davey Smith and the Connor twins. Philip, who everyone called Pip, had been her closest friend since they were little, having met while they were learning pickpocketing from Jack Reid. Jack found her as an orphan begging on the street and began teaching her the trade. But as she grew older, she wanted to do more honest work.

As children, she had always been Pip's protector. He was the closest thing to family Nell had. When she told Jack she wanted to find work honestly, she had expected Pip to follow. But he didn't. Now Pip worked in one of Jack's many groups of thieves who took by force. She barely saw him anymore, so she was pleased enough by the sight of her friend to step out of the shop.

"Morning, Nelly," Pip said, grinning up at her.

"Morning, Pip. What are you lot doing around here?"

"Didn't you see that toff inside?" Jimmy said.

She shrugged. "So?"

"You must be rustier than I thought," Davey said, leaning against the building. "If you can't spot a mark like that a mile away."

"I don't know about that one," she said slowly. "Seemed a little too fine, if you ask me."

Davey scoffed. "Too fine, indeed. Deep purses like that don't come wandering through our streets just any old time. Or haven't you noticed?"

"Of course I noticed," she retorted. "I may be rusty, but I'm not an idiot. What I'm saying is that one in there is too fine to be the type to carry his purse around with him. And he's far too fine to be a nobody."

Davey rolled his eyes. "I don't care if he's the Prince Regent, himself. Whatever he's got will put me in Jack's good graces for a month or more. I ain't about to pass that up."

"More fool you," she said.

"What do you mean, Nelly?" Pip said, crossing his arms. "What's got you keyed up?"

"Sweet on him, isn't she?" Jimmy said, elbowing Pip with a wink. Pip ducked his head.

Nell rolled her eyes. "Not likely. All I'm saying—"

It was a shame, really, that the gentleman came out when he did. Nell was pretty sure she had the boys close to her way of thinking. If he had stayed inside a few minutes more, she might have convinced them that he wasn't worth their time and she could have discreetly seen him to the respectable side of town. As it was, he came out before she'd finished having her say. He was holding several packages in one arm. Nell realized he had bought raw supplies, rather than packaged spells, which surprised her a little.

"Oh," the gentleman said brightly, as if he didn't have a care in the world. "Good day, friends. Pardon me, won't you?"

He made as if to scoot past their group, but Davey was blocking his way in an instant.

"Not so fast, gov'nor," he said smoothly.

Jimmy reached behind Nell and pulled the shop door shut.

"You look as if you've got quite a ways to travel," Davey continued. "I'm thinking your purse will be weighing you down a bit. Don't you think, lads?"

The Connor twins chuckled appreciatively.

Nell ought to have given the stranger up for lost and gone back inside, but she didn't. She couldn't explain why she was so determined to see him safe. Perhaps it had been the way he had easily accepted her as someone worthy of his time and respect. Or perhaps it was the cheerful way he greeted everyone, as if everyone he met was a friend.

Before she could think better of it, she stepped between Davey and the gentleman.

"What's this?" Davey said.

"Like I was telling you before," she said. "I think you should leave off this one."

Davey sneered. "Want him for yourself, do you?"

"You know I don't do that anymore."

"Told you she was sweet on him," Jimmy said.

Nell surreptitiously slipped her hand into her left pocket and palmed the sprig of rosemary. She eased her hand back out and did a little swishing motion by her side. "Come on now, Davey. You know me better than that. I don't think this one's a good idea."

She could tell the persuasion spell started to activate when Davey took a step back. "And why not?" he asked, belligerent.

She leaned forward as if imparting a big secret. "Don't ask why, but something about this one's manner tells me: judge's son. If you take this one, I'll bet you anything you'll be swinging within a fortnight."

"If they can catch me," Davey said, but he seemed a little less certain now.

"You think he came all this way without telling his pa where he went?" she persisted, grateful that the man in question hadn't been foolish enough to interrupt. She didn't dare look back at him to see how he was reacting. "Let this one off, Davey. He's not worth the risk."

The spell took hold of Pip first. He tugged on Davey's arm. "She's right. Let's go."

Davey's eyes darted between Nell and the gentleman. Finally, he relented. The group stalked off.

Nell pocketed the rosemary and grabbed the gentleman's wrist. "Come on, sir," she whispered. "Before they get wise."

With an expression that seemed equal parts amused and bemused, the gentleman complied.

When she reached the wider streets that marked the safer part of London, she rounded on the gentleman. "You know you almost had your throat slit," she said.

The statement did not have the effect she intended. The gentleman did not look at all horrified, mainly curious. "Indeed?" he said. "I daresay I'm in your debt then, aren't I, my dear?"

She frowned. "Not hardly. Just take care you don't go wandering around that part of town again. I can't guarantee I'll be there next time. Or that the spell will work again."

"Ah, so you *were* working magic." He seemed pleased to

have noticed. "What sort of spell was that? I can't say I've ever seen it before."

She huffed. "It's a persuasion spell. Now, if you'll excuse me, I'd better get back to my work."

"Oh, just a moment," he said, with a hand on her shoulder.

Nell sighed and turned around.

"Why did you stop them? Not that I'm not grateful, mind you. Simply curious. I'm not sure many would have bothered."

She wasn't entirely sure of the answer to the question, which made her uncomfortable. She shrugged. "Right thing to do, I suppose."

His mouth quirked. "How noble. Well, my dear. One good turn certainly deserves another. If you ever require my assistance, please do not hesitate to call. The name is Charles Kentworthy and I live at 16 Berkeley Square." He bowed to her as if she were a fine lady and walked away.

Nell stared at him, despite her need to head back to the shop. He really was a fool to give her his address. How could he know she wouldn't rob him? Overly trusting blighter. She supposed he wasn't entirely wrong to trust her, since she didn't plan to do anything with the information. He had given her his name, as if he considered her a friend. She was a little stunned by the whole interaction. She realized that she was reacting to him the way she expected him to react to her. Wasn't that just like the upper crust? To make her feel like he had done her a favor instead of the other way around.

"Well, where were you?" Mr. Smelting said when she finally walked back into the shop.

"That toff was lost. I helped him find his way back."

Smelting snorted. "I believe it. I don't think that one had been inside a spell shop in his life."

"What was he here for, then?"

"Oh, he bought a nice little bundle of ingredients. He

asked all sorts of questions about what each one was good for."

She rolled her eyes. "I'll bet you charged him double."

Smelting frowned suddenly. "No," he said slowly. "He was good at haggling, actually. Knew how much each ought to cost."

She was as surprised as Smelting was by this revelation. But she proceeded to go about her work and tried to put the tall, friendly Kentworthy person out of her mind.

CHAPTER 2

WHEN JACK first took her in, he had roomed her with a bunch of other rag-tag children in a long attic space above a butcher shop. The space was dark and musty and the smells of the butcher shop always leaked through the boards. Lumpy mattresses had been placed in neat rows, giving a narrow walkway if a person stepped one foot carefully in front of the other. She still lived in the attic space, as did many of the other thieves she worked with growing up.

Jack was a man who looked after his people. Anyone who worked for him knew they could go to him if they ever were short of money or food or a place to sleep. Jack always got them what they needed.

He was no charity house, of course. Everyone knew they'd have to pay him back. Nell had always liked that about Jack. It made her feel accomplished to finally repay him for everything he'd done over the years.

Pip still lived in the long room too, on the mattress next to hers. This, and the cost of living in London, were the primary reasons she still stayed there. Admittedly, she hardly ever saw Pip anymore, but he was waiting for her when she got home, sitting cross-legged on his mattress.

Where Nell was pale, with hair so blonde as to nearly be

white (though these days it was more of a dull grey color from grime and dirt), and light blue eyes, Pip had fawn-colored skin, dark curly hair, and brown eyes. Where Nell was tall, broad, and muscular, Pip was short and slim. He had grown up to be a very pretty sort of man: petite, with long lashes and pouting lips.

When Nell hit the right age, Jack started pressuring her to move to one of his harlot houses instead of pickpocketing. She used to wonder why Pip didn't get the same amount of pressure to work in a harlot house—anyone could see he'd be popular there—but it all made sense after she left Jack's employ and Jack took on Pip as his bedmate.

"What got into you today?" he said when she walked in.

"What do you mean?" she said, feigning ignorance.

He rolled his eyes. "You know what I mean. Why did you get yourself involved with that toffee-nosed blighter? He would have been an easy mark. I'll bet Davey wouldn't even have needed to hurt him to get his purse out."

Nell considered this for a moment. "I think you'd be surprised. He was an odd one."

"Well, I don't see why you should cut in like that. Davey was hopping mad afterwards. You'd better steer clear of him for a while."

"Thanks," she said.

"Don't bother thanking me yet. Just wait until Davey tells Jack."

"You think he's likely to?"

Pip sighed in exasperation.

"Right," she answered. "I guess I do owe Jack an explanation."

Pip didn't respond to this. He turned and started to pick at a loose thread on his mattress.

"You know," Nell said, watching him. "I'm not sure I like seeing you around the likes of Davey Smith."

Pip shrugged, still not looking at her. "It's what Jack tells me to do, so I do it."

"You sure it isn't because you're sweet on Jimmy Connor? Don't think I didn't notice how bashful you get around him."

Pip pursed his lips but didn't respond.

"You know the Connor twins are just as bad as Davey when it comes down to it," she pressed. "They're no good. You deserve better than Jimmy anyway. Are you unhappy with Jack? Is that the trouble? From what I hear you're his favorite now. I should think you'd be enjoying that."

Pip continued to pick at the thread silently.

"I'm only trying to look out for you," she said. After another long moment of silence, she sighed and said, "I suppose you don't need me looking out for you anymore, now that you have Jack to do that."

"Yeah," he said at last. "I guess that's so."

She watched him leave, wishing she'd been able to talk some sense into him. Pip never did have much sense where love was concerned. Pip's pining for Jimmy Connor only served to make him frustrated, but clearly it was useless to persuade him out of it.

Nell couldn't understand why Pip wasted his time wishing for someone else. She had never felt the sentimental pull that others did. She had no use for romance and it held no appeal. She enjoyed having a friend who could serve as a reliable bedmate when called upon. She was fairly sure Pip's needs were met as far as that was concerned, so to her mind, he had everything he could possibly want. When he had a lover as dedicated to him as Jack was, it seemed as though he was making himself unhappy unnecessarily.

She wished she could have expressed all of that to him more effectively. Ever since she had gone to work her odd-jobs, she had lost touch with her friend. Then again, maybe it wasn't her lookout, not anymore.

The next morning, Pip crept into the room—his empty bed

a sure sign that he had spent the night with Jack—and shook her awake.

"Jack's not pleased with you, Nelly."

Nell tried to ignore the twist in her gut at the thought of disappointing Jack—or worse, angering him.

"He wants to see me?"

"Not yet."

"Did he say when? I don't like the thought of him stewing about it."

"He's pretty busy right now. Training up a new group. I imagine he'll send me around when he's ready, though."

"Right," she said. "Thanks."

Pip chewed on his lip, staring at the ground. "Just make sure you don't try any more foolishness, all right? I'm no good at covering for you. Jack knows me too well for that."

She nodded and got ready for work while Pip slipped out as quietly as he had crept in.

Jack took his time tracking her down. She worked herself into a bundle of nerves wondering what he would say about her interference. When Pip finally came home one night and said, "Come on, Jack wants to talk to you now," she was almost relieved.

Jack Reid was old enough to be Nell's father. She didn't know his exact age (she didn't even know her own), but she knew him to be as spry on his feet as Davey and as nimble with his fingers as Pip. He was a tall man with broad shoulders, skin as pale as her own, short red hair, and bright blue eyes.

Jack had a small group of lovers who, if the rumors were true, had few complaints. For all his independence and power, Jack liked to have someone nestled beside him. In recent years, Pip had earned the honor of favorite. Any time Pip wasn't working, he was at Jack's side.

Jack was waiting for them at his usual tavern. It was where all of Jack's people came to give him their takes for the day. If it was money, he would pass back a percentage to the ones who had earned it. Stolen goods were examined and then put in a sack to be sold off later. Jack was sitting in the center of a bench with his back against a long wooden table, just as Nell remembered from her last visit years prior. He was going through a small bundle of goods piled up on the bench beside him.

"Well, if it isn't Nell," he said jovially and patted the bench on his other side. She took the seat as indicated, sitting with her back to the table too.

Jack reached for Pip's arm and pulled her friend onto his lap. Pip took his seat as easily as Nell had taken hers. He sat facing her and leaned his shoulder into Jack's chest.

"Let me finish with what Tom brought and I'll be right with you," he said, wrapping one arm around Pip's slim waist.

She nodded and he turned to sort through the items beside him. Finally, apparently satisfied, he reached for the sack on the table. Pip leaned forward to hold the sack open, which earned him a soft kiss on the temple. After Jack piled everything into the sack, he tucked it under the table and waved at the barmaid for drinks.

"How have you been keeping yourself?" he said, resting his arm across his lover's thighs and gazing studiously at Pip's profile.

She shrugged even though Jack wasn't looking at her. "Been all right," she answered. "Keeping busy."

He smiled and stroked Pip's curly hair idly. "Really? From what I hear, you've had time to spare."

"Oh?" she said.

The barmaid set three pints of ale on the table. Both Pip and Nell grabbed a mug, but Jack didn't even glance at the drinks. His focus was all on the young man in his lap. "Davey says he saw you hanging around old Smelting's store the other day."

She didn't want to argue with his word choice, even though she didn't agree with it, so she said nothing.

He grinned at her silence and kissed Pip's jaw. "He says you got in the way of a very important job."

She shifted in her seat. "Well, you know how Davey is. He'll say anything."

He tilted his head in acquiescence and moved his hand from Pip's hair to cup the back of his neck. "I'll admit I didn't believe him at first. You're not the type to interfere. Not usually. I wouldn't have believed it if the other lads hadn't backed up his story."

Nell glanced at Pip. He was looking resolutely into his mug, as if oblivious to both her glance and Jack's touch. It troubled her to see that he didn't seem to be enjoying his lover's attention. Was he pulling away from Jack as much as he was pulling away from her? She made a mental note to put more effort into checking on her friend. Perhaps he still needed her protection.

"'Course, they weren't all as forthcoming about it as Davey, were they?" Jack said, fingers sliding up and down Pip's neck.

Pip gave a little shiver and hunched forward.

Jack chuckled and kissed Pip on the neck. "We got it out of them in the end, though." He continued, still not looking at her, nuzzling Pip's neck as he spoke, "But what I want to know is why you have enough time on your hands to muck about with my boys when they're only doing what I tell them?"

She swallowed and set her mug down carefully. He was being direct, at least. She liked that about Jack. Best to make a clean breast of the matter. "I'll be honest, Jack. I didn't mean to."

He finally turned to look at her, arching an eyebrow.

She took a deep breath. "It won't happen again, I promise."

"You know that's not good enough, Nell."

"I know," she said. "What do you want?"

Jack looked pleased. "Those boys were tracking a very valuable mark. Davey thinks they could have gotten ten pounds off him."

"Ten—" She broke off. "He couldn't possibly have been carrying that much with him, Jack. You know that."

His look was direct. "And how much do you imagine that cloak was worth, and the coat, and the shoes? Not to mention whatever odds and ends that type always has about on their person: snuff boxes, pocket watches, rings, buckles? I know you've been out of the business a few years, Nell, but you know as well as I do that you stole away with a very valuable prize. Even if Davey was exaggerating."

She did know it.

"You owe me."

She knew that too. She ran a hand over her face. "All right," she said. "We'll call it ten, then?"

He nodded and slid his hand down Pip's back before reaching for his own mug of ale at last. "You know you've always been one of my favorites, Nell," he said, after taking a sip. "So, you can choose how you want to work it off. But not with your honest nonsense," he added with a smirk. "I'd like to be paid back this year, thank you very much."

It was an easy decision to make. She had no interest in working in a brothel, not when she knew she wouldn't have a choice in who her customers were. She had no interest in working as a thief either, but she felt more comfortable with that prospect. It was the devil she knew.

"Fine," she said. "I'll do what I used to. But, I should warn you, I'm a bit rusty."

He grinned. "I don't normally like my older ones picking pockets, but I'll make an exception in your case. You always were good. If you can't keep up, though, I'll have to move you to something else."

"Right."

"You know I like to be fair, so you'll get the usual cut, of course," he continued. "Don't want you starving on the job. Pip will make sure you remember the ropes and you two can pair up while you pay it off."

Pip beamed, dimpling adorably. "Like old times, eh, Nelly?"

Jack laughed and tousled Pip's hair. "Just like. It'll be good to see you two back together again."

And just like that, Nell found herself back in Jack Reid's employ.

CHAPTER 3

IF NELL WERE honest with herself, she would admit to being uncomfortable with how easily she slid back into her old lifestyle. It felt right to work with Pip again; almost like they belonged together, in some way.

Late in the morning, Pip would come by her mattress with information about whatever section of London Jack had assigned them for the day, and they would head into town. They'd work until dusk and then go back to the tavern with their takes. Nell had missed spending so much time with Pip. They worked well together. He was all charm and dimpled smiles, sweet pleas for a pence, and everyone was so taken with him that they didn't notice Nell sliding in and out of their personal space.

Back at the tavern, they'd dump all of their take on the table in front of Jack, who'd sort through it and take it to a seller to determine its value. A few days later, he'd divide the money between the three of them. Nell knew she ought to take a smaller cut in order to pay Jack back faster. But it was far too enjoyable going to bed less hungry each night, too easy to spend all day with Pip, and too gratifying to earn Jack's praise again, that she continued to pocket exactly what Jack doled out to her and no less.

She began to fret that she was losing sight of what she'd once been working towards, so she assuaged some of her worries by investing in some ingredients from Smelting's shop. She had a vague notion that if she could get really good at magic, she could work out a way to get out of her current life, although she had no idea how to learn it or what sort of jobs were even possible.

The first challenge was finding time to practice. So many people shared the long room that she never had any privacy. And Nell didn't like the idea of other people learning she could do magic. It felt private, a secret key that she wasn't willing to share. She hid her materials under her mattress and waited for the brief moments where she could steal in a practice. It was difficult to improve on the persuasion and look-away spells by herself, so she put off working on those.

One night the room was almost empty and those who were in it were asleep, so she chanced practicing the spell to make things weightless. It had been giving her some stick. She was so focused on levitating a bit of string that she didn't even notice when Pip sat down on his own mattress behind her.

"Blimey," he whispered.

Nell dropped the spell and stuffed the materials into her pocket.

"Where'd you learn that?" he asked.

"I've been watching street magicians and old Smelting."

"Can you teach me?"

She didn't answer. She wasn't entirely sure she could teach him. And besides, she wasn't sure she wanted to. She liked Pip, but she didn't like the idea of her magic being used for crime. Instead she said, "Why are you home so early?"

He shrugged, folding his legs up under him. "Molly was on his lap. I figure I have the evening free."

"Really?" Nell said, surprised. "Can't remember the last

time that happened. You've been going to bed with him every night for a while now."

"Months. And months." He gave a small huff. "You know, I always knew Jack to have a whole string of lovers at a time. But in the past few years, it feels like it's only me."

"Well, that's a good thing, isn't it? I fancy that's some sort of honor. Jack isn't easily impressed, you know. I should think you'd be pleased."

He chewed his lip and then said suddenly, "Can you show me how to do that bit with the string?"

"Well, if you've got the evening free, why don't we go for a pint?" she said, hoping to distract him.

He grinned and they hurried into the night, the materials still in her pocket, since she hadn't had a chance to hide them away.

The tavern was busy and they had to push through the crowd to get to the bar. With pints in hand, they started looking for seats. Nell spotted Molly standing among the crowd, flirting with a sailor.

"I thought you said Molly was with Jack tonight."

Pip looked around until he spotted Molly. He cursed silently. "Hold this," he said, handing her his pint. Then he slipped away through the crowd.

Nell watched as he approached the blonde, who talked briefly with him before taking the sailor by the arm and walking out. Pip then wound his way through the tavern until he reached a gaming table. Nell recognized Jack's ginger hair among the players. Pip leaned down to whisper in Jack's ear. Jack cupped Pip's neck while he listened, then glanced over his shoulder until he caught sight of Nell. Finally, he nodded at Pip and chucked him under the chin. Pip made his way back to Nell.

"What was all that about?"

He took his pint without a word and took a long pull.

"Molly's working after all. Told me to keep him company. Thank God, there's a seat. Hurry."

He grabbed her wrist and dragged her to a table where a couple was just getting up. They squeezed onto the bench together. There wasn't much space, so Pip sat astride the bench, leaning his elbow on the table.

"I asked if I could sit with you for a bit. He'll join us when he's done."

Feeling crowded, Nell rotated on the bench so she faced the table. They sat together in companionable silence and waited for Jack to join them. Nell didn't even see him approach until he was stepping on the bench and swinging around to sit on the table in front of Pip. He scooped up Pip's pint and took a sip. After placing it back on the table, he gave them both a beneficent smile.

"Damn me, it's good to see you two like this again. You work well together, you know."

"We do," Pip said. "I've missed this."

Jack grinned and ran a hand through Pip's hair, gently pulling him to lean back against his leg. "I know you have."

Pip's eyes closed at the petting.

Nell didn't respond, taking a sip of her drink instead. It made her uneasy with how comfortable they were all getting with the current arrangement. Didn't they know it was temporary, until she paid Jack back?

"Since when do you stuff your pockets like a magpie, Nell?" Jack said. He flipped his hand open and dumped her materials on the table.

Nell slapped at her pocket, realizing too late that Jack had picked it. She cursed herself for not noticing, but wasn't surprised to discover that Jack was still as good at his craft as he was when she was little. He did teach her everything she knew.

He picked up a feather and twirled it between his thumb and forefinger. "What is all this for anyhow?"

Pip tilted his head to look up at Jack. "Did you know she can do magic?"

She cursed herself again. She should have warned him off telling Jack. She wasn't ready for people to know yet. Although Pip could hardly be faulted for not knowing that. Nell didn't usually keep secrets, especially not from him.

Jack turned his keen gaze on her. "You looking to be a street magician, Nell?"

"Hardly," she said.

"She was floating bits of string when I walked into the room today," Pip continued.

She gestured at the feather still in Jack's hand. "It's a work in progress."

Jack looked confused. "What is it you're aiming for then? People like us aren't spellcasters. That sort of thing takes money and learning."

She shrugged. "I don't know," she said.

"So you're learning to float bits of string," he continued. "You're wanting to use it when you go back to your odd-job work? Is that it?"

"No," she said. "That isn't it either. I think magic might be my way to get out of...all of this."

He raised an eyebrow and handed her the feather.

Nell didn't like the incredulous look Jack was giving her, particularly when she had just voiced something important. "I know it sounds ridiculous," she said. "But I think I'm good. Or I could be good. In fact I'm sure of it. It isn't just floating bits of string. There's other stuff I'm learning too."

Jack stroked Pip's hair while he gave her a pensive look. "You know," he said at last, "I've been wondering how you managed to needle the boys into letting that toff go."

Pip looked up at Jack in surprise. "You mean she used magic on us?"

Jack continued running his fingers through Pip's hair, but kept his eyes fixed on Nell.

She sighed. "I already told you I didn't mean to. I didn't think it would work, to be honest."

"What sort of spell was it?" Jack asked.

"Persuasion."

"That's not on!" Pip said.

"I'm sorry." She glanced up at Jack but he didn't look angry, more thoughtful. He took another sip of Pip's drink.

"Could be a useful skill," he said at last. "Persuasion. You say you're still learning. I might have a talk with old Smelting. See if there's anything he could teach you."

"Really?"

"Like I said, could be useful. I wouldn't be opposed to funding the effort, as it were. Especially if I got a good return on it."

"I don't know," she hedged.

He drained the rest of the pint and handed it to Pip. "Go get us another," he said, tweaking one of Pip's dark curls.

Pip walked off to do as he was told.

Jack leaned forward and lowered his voice. "Think about it," he said. "I like having you back, Nell. You always were one of my best. If you can do magic on top of everything else..." He shrugged expressively. "We could have it made. Besides," he added, looking across the crowd in the direction Pip had walked. "He's happier working with you. I don't like to tell you, but I've been worried about him. Having you around, it helps. Always has."

She sighed. "I know."

"I took each of you in—what? Twenty years ago? You could barely string sentences together and Pip was so scrawny as to look your age, for all that he's a couple years older. I've known you both almost all your lives and I've never seen two people so different and yet so much alike. You both fight for people first, and...I don't know...principles. Money always comes last for you. I don't know anyone else like that." He paused and gave her a fatherly sort of smile.

"It's why you two get on so well. Always thought so. I could have you well set up to work together forever, look after each other the way you do."

She knew he meant it.

"Just think about it," he said. "I'll talk to Smelting tomorrow and see what he says. If he thinks he can teach you, I'll even pay for the lessons."

"Not really?"

"Would you do it?"

"Maybe," she said, her mind whirring. She had always prided herself on repaying Jack. She did not like to add on to her debt. She considered magic her escape from this world. Then again, continuing to work with Pip and to keep him safe…it felt like where she belonged.

She was so distracted mulling over Jack's offer that she didn't notice Davey until he was leaning over the table and practically growling at her. "I should have never listened to you. Imagine telling me to let that toff go. And here you are, calm as you please, back in the game. I should've known it was all a bloody trick."

Jack wasted no time in taking control of the situation. He laid a reassuring hand on Nell's shoulder before stepping off the table. "Come on, Davey. Let's talk."

"It ain't fair, Jack."

"I know, Davey, I know. Let me explain."

She watched Jack guide Davey a little ways away by the wall. Jack was cool and unfazed in the face of Davey's anger. She watched in amazement as Davey gradually calmed down and even started to look cheered by the conversation.

Pip came back with another pint. "Where'd he go?"

Nell pointed with her chin at the two men standing by the wall.

"Should I wait for him, do you think?" Pip wondered aloud.

"He's talking to Davey; he might need the drink now," she said.

Pip snorted and walked away to join them.

Jack grinned as his lover approached, swinging an arm around Pip's shoulders and kissing his cheek. He continued his talk with Davey for a few minutes more, pressing Pip to his side, and then, to Nell's surprise, took the pint from Pip and passed it to Davey. Davey laughed and walked away, clearly in better spirits.

Jack watched him go and then tilted Pip's chin up and spoke in a low voice. It occurred to Nell suddenly that Jack might be training Pip to take over his position one day. It would explain why she only saw Pip when they were working; he was forever in Jack's company. She felt saddened by this realization for it meant that when she eventually left again, she would probably have to leave Pip, possibly forever.

This line of thought was interrupted by the sight of Jack bracketing Pip against a wall and pinning him with a long and heated kiss, Pip grasping Jack's shoulders. Perhaps she needn't worry about her friend so much; he was clearly in good hands.

"Back in the fold, are you, Nell?" someone said beside her. She turned to find Jimmy Connor taking a seat next to her on the bench.

"For the time being."

Jimmy grinned. "I'll bet Pip's glad of it."

"Yeah," she said. "I think he is."

She glanced at her friend to find that Jack now had one long leg pressed up between Pip's and was kissing up and down his lover's neck. The noise had died down a bit nearby, in part because of the spectacle, and she could hear Pip's moans and gasps from where she sat. She couldn't entirely make out the words he was saying, but she thought she caught hints of *Jack* and *please*. She wondered when her usually quiet friend had developed a taste for public affection. She supposed it was Jack's influence.

Beside her, Jimmy snickered. "Oy!" He yelled. "Go on and take your boy home, Jack! Or are you trying to make the rest of us jealous?"

Everyone around them chuckled appreciatively, including Jack, who laughed loudly into the crook of Pip's neck and seemed to push up against him with more intensity. Pip whimpered and his knuckles went white around Jack's shirt fabric.

Nell felt a small stirring at the sight. It had been a while since she'd looked after her own needs.

"They do love to put on a show, those two. Don't know that I've seen Jack trot anyone out like he does our Pip. Almost makes me want to find a little something for myself tonight," Jimmy muttered, inadvertently echoing her thoughts. He was scratching his chin and watching the couple with unabashed interest. "What about you?"

"Not a bad idea. Think I'll go do that. Thanks, Jimmy," she said, patting his back.

As she turned to walk away, Jimmy grumbled loudly, "Damn me, Nell. I was trying to proposition you."

She laughed over her shoulder. "You're not to my taste."

He heaved a dramatic sigh. She left, confident that Pip, panting in his lover's arms, did not need her to say goodnight.

She strolled through the narrow alleyways in the fading light. It was early yet, and seeing two people so thrilled by each other's touch had created a hunger in her to find something similar for herself. Jimmy saying the desire out loud had acted like a stamp of approval.

It had been a while, if she was honest. She had been so busy with her odd-jobs before that she was often too exhausted to keep late nights. Not that she deprived herself, exactly. Nell was very attuned to what she wanted, in all aspects of her life. But survival had taken some amount of precedence over pleasure. She knew exactly where she wanted to fulfill the need and hoped that door would still be open to her, after months of neglect.

Patience Carew had been another one of the many children Jack had picked up. She was older than both Nell and Pip and, when she was old enough, Jack moved her from pickpocketing to work in one of his brothels. She had been quite popular at the start of her career there and, from what Nell could gather, she seemed to prefer it to pickpocketing.

"Less skulking about," Patience used to tell her. "People know what they're in for when they see me now. Well," she had added with a smirk, "They think they know what they're in for. I like to think they're always pleasantly surprised by the end."

Then Patience got pregnant, and her work was naturally put on hold. When she made the rare decision to keep the baby, Jack arranged to have someone watch it for her when she went back to the brothel, which Nell had always thought was remarkably decent of him. But then Patience had her second baby and decided to give up that line of work. Jack found her a job as a barmaid and, although she made less money, she reduced the risk of increasing her small brood. Of course, from what Nell had heard, Patience's old training didn't hurt; she managed to get the best tips out of her customers and she was very sly as to the hows.

Nell wasn't sure if the children would still be up, so she knocked softly on her friend's door. A small girl, who looked much like Patience had as a child, opened the door.

"My name's Nell," Nell said. "Is your mother in?"

The child didn't have to answer because Patience herself came to stand behind her. She was a gorgeous woman with dark red hair that fell in wavy tendrils from where she'd pulled it back. She was almost as tall as Nell, with an enticingly curvy figure, pale skin, large blue eyes, and full lips. She arched her eyebrows at the sight of Nell and quickly turned her attention to her daughter.

"All right, Matty," she said, "go on and go to bed now. Scoot." She gave her daughter a little smack on the bum as the girl ran off. Then she leaned against the door jamb and crossed her arms. "Well, well. Ain't it been an age?"

"You busy?"

Patience snorted. "And ain't it a fine evening? I'm doing very well, thank you kindly for asking. And yes, the little ones are growing up so fast. Such a wonder."

Nell rolled her eyes. "Sorry."

Patience's mouth quirked. "Eh, you were never one to mince words. Only I can't remember the last time you came around."

"It's been a while."

"Found someone else, have you? What's she like?"

"Oh now, you know that was never our way," Nell said, sliding a hand around Patience's waist. "No conditions we said, remember?" Patience's smile was coy. "Besides, I've been far too busy to find someone else."

Patience laughed and leaned forward for a kiss.

Nell closed the space between them, cupping Patience's cheek with her other hand. A whistle echoed through the night air, coming from down the street.

Patience broke off the kiss, but took Nell's hand. "Oh, come on in then," she said. "We got to be quiet, though. They're little but they got big ears."

CHAPTER 4

THE NEXT DAY, true to his word, Jack talked to Smelting about teaching Nell magic. When she and Pip brought their takes back to him that evening, he told her about it.

"He says he's interested, but wants to know what you can do first. He's coming by tonight."

"Tonight?"

Jack nodded. "I told him what all you had in your pockets and he said he'd bring those supplies to see what you could do with 'em."

"I'm not sure I like the idea of everyone watching, Jack."

He rolled his eyes. "Then we'll go up to my place. Will you do it?"

She considered for a moment and then nodded. Jack ordered her a pint and she nursed it, torn between wanting to guzzle the whole thing down out of nerves and fearing what the drink would do to her magical ability. She was incredibly anxious about performing in front of a real spellcaster.

Jack pulled Pip onto his lap and they kept her company while she waited for Smelting to arrive. She could tell Pip had noticed her nervousness. He kept trying to distract her with chatter.

After a couple of hours, Smelting arrived with a small satchel of ingredients.

"We're going upstairs to my place," Jack said. "She doesn't want an audience."

Smelting snorted. "And here I was thinking I'd get a free drink out of the bargain."

Jack grinned. "Who said you wouldn't? I'll get you one after."

Thus mollified, Smelting agreed.

Jack took Pip's hand and led the way to his little flat, located above the tavern. It was a small space with a rickety table and a large bed. Pip sat down on the bed, seeming perfectly at home. He fussed a little at the coverlet, trying to get it to lay flat. Jack sat next to him and tugged him close to kiss his temple, then pulled Pip's head to lean against his shoulder.

Nell felt as if she was intruding on their privacy, but she pushed that thought out of her head. She was just grateful she didn't have to perform magic in front of the whole tavern. Smelting dumped the contents of the bag onto the table.

"All right," he said. "Let's see what you can do."

She started with the levitation spell, since they'd already talked about it.

Smelting sniffed, looking unimpressed. "Not a bad attempt, I suppose. Anything else?"

She tried the persuasion spell, trying to get Smelting to hand her the feather on the table. It took some doing, as it had with the men in front of the shop, but she managed to get him to do it eventually.

"That's pretty good," Smelting said. "Could use a bit of work, of course. Your hand gestures need to be more precise."

"Well, I did teach myself," she said with huff.

"Anything else?" he said.

She cast the look-away spell. Like the persuasion spell, it took a few tries to get right. She heard Pip stir on the bed, as if startled, when she finally succeeded in getting Smelting to be distracted from looking at her.

Smelting seemed intrigued after she was done. "What was that one?"

She allowed a bit of pride to leak into her voice. "It's a look-away spell. I worked it out when I was trying to learn invisibility. I can't do invisibility yet," she added hastily. "But I thought it was pretty good."

Smelting frowned as if he didn't like how impressed he was. "It's more than pretty good," he said. "You've gone and made up a new spell."

"Do you think she has talent then?" Jack said.

"I'd say so. She needs precision. But I could teach her that."

"Same rate you gave me this afternoon?"

"Yes, that offer still stands." He shook his head a little. "Blow me, that look-away spell is something else, though. You could certainly put that one to good use."

Nell grinned.

"And here I was thinking magic was a useless thing for her to learn," Jack said, getting off the bed. "How long before she can use those spells on a job?"

Smelting shrugged. "Depends on the job, I suppose. You need to tighten your motions," he said to her. "That's the reason you're not getting consistent results." He made a crude imitation of her own hand gestures. "You're all flopsy. But if you practice at it, you could be good enough to go at it sooner rather than later."

Jack clapped him on the shoulder. "Very good. What do you think, Nell?"

Nell considered. Her dreams were so close to her reach. "Can I think about it?"

"Of course," Jack said generously. "Think about it. I'll pay Smelting here to teach you as soon as you say the word."

"Thank you, Jack."

"As I said," he said, guiding them toward the door. "I look after my own." He opened the door and turned to Pip. "Come along, Pip. We don't want to be late."

Pip winced. "Oh," he said. "That's tonight, isn't it?"

"What's tonight?" Nell said, following Smelting downstairs.

"Oh, Pip and I have an appointment," Jack said. "Just want to get Smelting that pint before we go."

They went back into the tavern, and Jack left Pip and Nell by the door to go buy Smelting his promised pint.

"What's this appointment for?" Nell said.

Pip shrugged, his eyes on the ground. "Something Jack wants me to do."

"Is Jack teaching you his work?"

Pip gave a humorless little laugh. "I imagine Jack's teaching me everything he knows."

"You don't seem very happy about it."

Before Pip could answer, Jack walked up, and cupped Pip's chin, tilting it up to meet his face. He pressed a soft kiss to his lips. "Don't look so frightened, boy," he chided in a gentle voice. "Don't I always take care of you?"

Pip closed his eyes and nodded.

Jack kissed the side of Pip's mouth. "Come along then," he whispered. Then he turned to Nell. "Practice," he said, pointing a finger at her. "And think about my offer."

She grinned. "I will. Thank you, Jack."

He gave her a smile, put a careful arm around Pip's shoulders, and guided him out of the tavern.

Nell leaned against the side of the door, watching them go. It was strange to have her theories confirmed about Jack teaching Pip his side of the business. But she did wonder what on earth made Pip so nervous about it. Didn't he want to take over when Jack was done? Pip had been somewhat morose of late. He'd always been quiet, but never quite so moody. Perhaps he wasn't overly fond of public affection after all. Had his pining for Jimmy Connor reached new heights? Was there something else?

She sighed and pushed herself upright. She needed to practice, but first she needed to get Pip's problems out of her head. She strode to Patience's house.

Patience opened the door and gave her a little grin. "Back again, is it? They're still up, you know. You'll have to wait."

Nell shrugged. "Just wanted company. Fancy getting a pint with me?"

Patience grimaced. "I wish I could." She glanced over her shoulder. "Bit difficult these days, you know."

"Can't you find someone to watch them for you?"

"Who, for instance?"

"I don't know. I'm sure Jack could help you find someone."

Patience rolled her eyes. "I'm sure he could and then I'd have another year's worth of debts to pay for. No, thank you. I'll just do without the pint tonight. You're welcome to come in, if you'd like. They'll be going to bed in an hour or so."

But Nell didn't want to sit in a quiet house, watching Patience put her children to bed. She wanted to be somewhere noisy, where she could put her worries about Pip and her uncertainty over Jack's offer out of her mind. She shook her head. "Maybe another time."

Patience looked hurt, but said, "Thanks for thinking of me, all the same."

Nell gave her friend a quick kiss and left. She went back to the tavern and bought herself a pint. The noise around her did little to distract her, though. Finally, she went back to her mattress to make good on her promise to practice.

She wrestled with Jack's offer for several days. If she got some real training, she might find a way to make an honest living. On the other hand, accepting the offer would put her even more in his debt and she didn't want to think about how long it would take to pay him back.

Jack didn't broach the subject again for over a week. Pip was quiet on the topic as well, making Nell begin to wonder if the two men had forgotten. That is, until she and Pip met up with Jack after a particularly thin day. She suspected something was up when Jack didn't criticize the meager takes. He scooped up the dented pocket watch they had snagged and considered it.

"How's your practice coming along?"

She was surprised by the sudden change of topic. "I've been working on it."

He pulled a small pouch out of his pocket and dumped it on the table. "I went to Smelting to get more of the supplies you used. Care to show me?"

She glanced around the tavern, self-conscious.

He rolled his eyes. "No one's here yet. And besides, the point of the spell is to make people *not* notice you. Go on."

She did as she was told. Scooping up the rosemary, she did the complex gesture, remembering Smelting's advice to tighten her wrist. It took her a couple of tries, but she succeeded faster than she had in the past.

Jack gave a low whistle. "You have been practicing." He tossed the pocket watch he'd been holding on to the table. "How do you feel about a change of pace?"

"What do you mean?" Nell asked.

"I've been offered a big job. It would mean a nice-sized take for everyone involved."

"What is it?" Pip said.

Jack glanced between them. "It's a house job."

"But we've never done a burglary before," Pip said, looking worried.

"Wouldn't Davey be better suited to that? Or Tom?" Nell said.

"I'll send Tom with you to make sure you get in, since neither of you have broken into a house before. But once you're inside, it'll be even easier than picking a pocket."

Nell narrowed her eyes. "What aren't you telling us, Jack? Why us?"

He paused. "We're robbing a spellcaster."

Nell's first instinct was to panic. Robbing a spellcaster's house? Was she ready for such a bold move? "I don't know," she said. "He'll have spells and traps and—"

"You don't have to decide right now," he said, cutting her off. "I want you to think about it. Practice tonight, if it makes you think better. But if I take the job, I want you to go tomorrow night. The gentleman in question is supposed to be out of the house at that time."

Nell puffed out her cheeks in an exhale. "I'll think about it."

"The way I figure it," Jack went on, "even if someone is in that house, you can use your fancy new look-away spell until you can both get out. Smelting said he hadn't seen anything like it."

Nell couldn't help the glow of pride this reminder gave her. "All right," she said. "I'll practice tonight and let you know in the morning."

"Good girl," he said, clapping her on the back. "I'll get Smelting to give me some fresh ingredients for you if you do go in. And Pip can go back to your room and help you practice."

Pip nodded, eager. Jack pulled the young man in for a swift kiss and whispered instructions to come back home later that night.

Nell wondered idly how long Pip had considered Jack's little room his home.

She and Pip walked back to their shared living quarters. Pip watched her practice, telling her promptly when her spell was and wasn't working. She wasn't entirely sure how he was able to tell, other than the fact that he must have been concentrating very hard on noticing her. Finally, she was able to get the spell right on the first try every time.

With that, Pip pronounced himself satisfied and duly went home to Jack.

The next day, feeling bold, she told Jack she was ready. "What's the item we're looking for?"

"Simplest thing in the world. It's a quizzing glass. The gentleman keeps it in his study."

"How would we know what that looks like?"

"It's where he practices his magic. I expect you'll recognize what that looks like better than me."

She considered. She knew she ought to be put off by the information, but the prospect of seeing a proper spellcaster's workspace made her more keen to take the job than she had been before. "All right," she said at last.

"Pip says you were doing very well on the spell last night. Show me?"

He handed her another packet of ingredients, clearly anticipating her acceptance of the job. She pulled out the rosemary. As she had on the night before, she was able to get it on the first try, multiple times.

Jack was thrilled with the results. "Can you make it work on the two of you?"

"I can try." She pulled Pip in front of her and this time she held the rosemary sprig in front of his chest and made the motion in front of both of them. To her surprise, it worked. She tried again with Pip standing directly behind her and it still worked, although not as well.

Jack clapped his hands. "You're brilliant, Nell. Do you know that? Why, this is wonderful," he said. "I'll get Tom to take you tonight. We've been watching the house. We expect the gentleman to leave his house around eight and stay out until the early hours of the morning. So I want you heading over there no earlier than ten, maybe as late as midnight, just to be safe."

She was pleased by his praise but a trifle nervous at the upcoming challenge. "Right."

"Don't go and work yourself up now," Jack said. "If you get too nervous and think too hard, you'll make mistakes." He leaned in. "If you do this, I'll give you five pounds each."

Pip gasped. "Five? A piece?"

"Well?"

"I'm game to try," she said. She looked at Pip. It was plain as day from his expression that he was willing to risk it too. By way of an answer, she carefully picked up all of the magical ingredients, placed them back into the packet, and stowed them in her pocket.

Jack clapped her on the back and pulled Pip in for a kiss.

CHAPTER 5

THAT NIGHT, as promised, Tom took them to the fancy side of town after midnight, helped them break in through a back window, and then waited outside, keeping a lookout. She had wondered at Jack's insistence that Pip join, but it became clear when they reached the study door and he pulled out a lock-picking kit.

"Where did you learn that?" she hissed as he focused on the lock, tongue sticking out in his concentration.

"Where do you think? Jack taught me, of course," he whispered back.

"He really is teaching you everything he knows," she said.

"Told you," he said. "This was one of the more enjoyable lessons." He worked at the lock and then finally grinned. "Got it."

He paused, frowning, and pressed his palm to the door.

"What is it?" she asked.

"Something's...tugging at me," he said, his eyes wide. "Can't you feel it?"

She shook her head, wishing he'd hurry. She was getting anxious to go in and see a real spellcaster's workroom.

He swept his hand along the base of the door. "It gets

stronger down here," he breathed. "It wants to pull me in, I think."

She pulled out her rosemary and did the look-away spell.

He relaxed a little. "I think that helped."

"Did it go away?"

"No. But it...eased a little. Like a whisper more than a shout. Should we give it a go?"

She nodded. Carefully, slowly, he opened the door. But as it swung open, he braced himself against the door jamb.

"What's wrong?" she hissed, grabbing his arm.

"I—I don't think we should go in."

"Trapped?"

"I don't know. I've never felt anything like this before. I don't trust it."

She was just about to suggest going in by herself when she heard voices echoing down the stairs and saw a glimmer of candlelight. She dragged Pip backward, into the room where they had entered. There was a large piano on one side of the room and they scooted under it and crouched in the dark, waiting. Nell had to hunch forward to keep her head from hitting the bottom of the piano.

The voices paused at the study door.

"Strange," one man said. "They really didn't go inside. I wonder..."

Frantic, without thinking, she shoved Pip back a little so she could scoot in front of him and perform the look-away spell.

Suddenly, a man stood in the doorway to the room, silhouetted against the candlelight in the hall. He was round and looked to be about average height, although it was hard to tell from where she knelt on the floor. They waited, hoping he would turn and go away, and Nell continued to twist her wrist for the look-away spell.

"I have absolutely no plans tonight, m'dears," the man said. "So if you really want to sit there in the dark room until morning, do be my guests." Nell was astonished that the man's tone was colored with amusement. He leaned forward a bit, as if to get a better look. "Ah, under the piano, are we? Well, well. That does not seem comfortable."

Another figure came to stand next to the first one, taller and slimmer but with broad shoulders. "Good heavens, Bertie. What a terrible host you are, to keep your friends sitting in the dark like this."

"I know, darling, I know," said the first one—Bertie, Nell assumed. "But what can I say? People will drop in on me without any notice. How is one to prepare?"

They stood for a moment, at an impasse.

Finally, Bertie spoke again. "I do hate to criticize, but I think you should know that whatever spell you're attempting to do, m'dear, is simply not working."

Nell dropped her hand to her side. She glanced over her shoulder at Pip, who looked frightened but just as confused as she was. He shrugged. Taking that to mean that she was in charge of making decisions, Nell took a deep breath and crawled forward.

"Lovely," Bertie said, clapping his hands together. "Do come in, darlings. Let's go into the study, shall we? Much more comfortable for entertaining surprise guests."

The second man led the way, so all Nell could see was his tall, broad back. The first man, Bertie, brought up the rear. Nell dared a glance at him as she shuffled past. He was clearly a dandy of some sort, with an elegant brocade coat and an intricately knotted cravat. He smiled at her as if she were an honored guest and not a thief caught mid-burglary.

As they strode into the study, the dimly lit room was suddenly as bright as if it were daytime. Once inside, Nell was overwhelmed. There was a velvet cushioned settee, a huge mahogany desk with assorted materials scattered across it, a couple of wingback chairs, a globe, and a wide empty space of flooring. Lining the room were tall shelves filled with books, jars, and boxes. Nell recognized some of the materials and tools as similar to what Mr. Smelting used in his backroom, only of much finer quality.

"Please do be seated," Bertie said from behind, pointing to the wingback chairs.

It wasn't until they had perched cautiously on the edges of their seats that Nell got a good look at the second gentleman. He was seating himself on the settee, looking more at home than when they had last met. It was Charles Kentworthy, the toff she had rescued in front of Smelting's shop, the reason she was indebted to Jack in the first place and, in a way, the reason she was in the house at all.

She didn't have long to wonder if he would recognize her. He saw her and smiled in acknowledgement. "We meet again."

"Good heavens, Charlie, you don't mean to say you know our young friends?"

"You remember when I went to buy ingredients for Miss Hartford?"

"My soul, not the little guardian angel creature you told me about?"

"The very same."

"Will wonders never cease?"

Nell did not understand their attitudes. She was grateful that she was not being immediately handed over to the magistrate, but she was at a loss in how to respond to such breezy friendliness. "You're not angry?" she said at last.

Bertie tutted. "Well, all you have done so far, dear girl, is break into my house. Of course, I vastly prefer that guests use the front door, you understand, but I have yet to ascertain what it is you are doing here. I can hardly be angry until I've discovered that."

She stared. Were all toffs as blithely unworried as these two?

Now that he was standing in better lighting, she could see

more of her host than his size and the fineness of his clothing. He was pale with light brown hair, grey eyes, and a mouth that quirked up at the corners. She had first supposed him to be an older gentleman, but looking at him now, she realized he couldn't be much older than the Kentworthy bloke, if at all. Though he was at ease with himself in a manner most people didn't attain until they were older. She found herself intrigued despite her worry.

"And of course," he went on, "you rescued my dear friend here, which was simply too sweet of you. I do love gallantry, even when it is unnecessary. Especially then," he added as an afterthought.

"I'm sorry," she said, catching on to what he had said. "What do you mean when it's unnecessary? You do realize they were going to rob him, at least? I wouldn't put it past Davey to have slit his throat just to be spiteful."

"Well, I would hardly be a good friend if I sent Charlie without a protection spell, would I?" he said, as if it were the most obvious thing in the world.

She gaped.

"You mean Nell didn't even need to step in? After all that?" Pip said, finding his voice at last.

"That's exactly what I mean, darling," Bertie responded, beaming at Pip as if he had said something brilliant. "My heavens, where are my manners? Allow me to introduce myself. I am Viscount Finlington and this is my friend, Mr. Kentworthy. I take it you're Nell," he said, glancing at her, "and I did not catch your name, dear."

"Pip," he mumbled, clearly awed.

"Pip," the viscount said, bowing. "A pleasure indeed. I hope you don't mind my saying so, but you are the most adorable creature I have ever met."

Pip looked down at his shoes.

"Stop teasing the poor man, Bertie," Mr. Kentworthy reprimanded gently.

"Oh, I'm sure he gets it all the time, Charlie. He's far too pretty not to. But you're right of course. I do hope you will forgive me, Pip dear. It's a terrible habit of mine, truly. I say the most appalling things. Can't seem to stop myself." He gave Pip a beatific smile.

Pip peeked up at the man shyly.

Lord Finlington looked momentarily dazed from the glance. Then he seemed to shake himself mentally and leaned against the desk. "Now that we all know one another, let's get down to business, shall we? I do so hate to be inquisitive, but what are you sweet things doing in my house in the middle of the night?"

A look at Pip told Nell that she'd have to do the talking. She decided to go with honesty; the gentlemen were treating them so kindly, it seemed a crime not to be honest. Besides, she hoped that Mr. Kentworthy would put in a good word for her if they were sent to prison.

"We were on a job, sir," she said at last. "We were sent to find something."

The viscount raised an eyebrow but did not reply.

"Some sort of quizzing glass in your study."

He flipped open a box on his desk and pulled out a gold quizzing glass, allowing the chain to drape between his fingers. "The curse of the rich, I suppose," he said. "Having things that other people want. You don't happen to know who sent you to find this, do you, m'dear?"

She shook her head. She had a feeling he didn't mean Jack, but the man who had hired Jack in the first place, and Jack had never said who that was.

"Pity." He dropped the quizzing glass back into the box. "So." He hopped onto the desk, crossed his legs, and clasped his knee. "You came in here to get my quizzing glass and you even managed to open the door," he said, with a curious look at Pip, "but you didn't come inside. Why?"

"Well, Pip felt a sort of tugging," Nell ventured. "We

weren't sure if we should trust it."

Lord Finlington's eyes narrowed. "Indeed?"

"It seemed like a trap," she said. "He felt it before we opened the door, but I guess it got stronger after. I tried a look-away spell on it, but it wasn't strong enough."

"Ah, the rosemary," he said, as if he had just discovered the answer to a riddle. "Of course. What a clever notion. May I?" He held his hand out.

She hesitated and then dropped the now crumpled rosemary sprig into his palm.

He held it delicately between thumb and forefinger, sniffed it, and then examined it. "Sadly wilted little thing, isn't it? You know, rosemary does not have particularly good reusability. It loses potency far too quickly. Well," he said, carefully placing the sprig on the desk behind him. "Not to worry, m'dears. I'm sure you'll do better next time. Of course," he added, "I would vastly prefer if you didn't try my house again. Not that I wouldn't love to see you, you understand. It just gets a tad incommodious."

"You're not going to turn us in?" Pip said.

Lord Finlington tilted his head, looking sympathetic. "Well, I'm sure it is the done thing. But I do so hate to see good talent go to waste."

Nell frowned. She didn't know what the viscount was talking about. All he knew of them was their botched burglary attempt.

He noticed her expression and smiled, leaning back a bit. "Do you know, Nell dear, that I have over a dozen protection spells on this house? I knew the moment the window was open and the second your feet hit the floor. I was aware when you approached my study, when you got past the spell on the lock, and when you neatly avoided one of the traps I had laid to lure you in and catch you."

"There was a spell on the lock?" Pip said, sounding scared.

Lord Finlington gave him a small smile. "Yes, darling man, there was. You did the lock, I take it?"

Pip frowned, clearly unsure whether or not to own up to it.

The viscount laughed. "And a splendid job you did too. So adorably clever. Upon my soul, I've never in my life met a more intriguing pair of miscreants. And I do so love intrigue. Don't you agree, Charlie?"

Mr. Kentworthy chuckled. "Do have pity on them, Bertie. Look at their faces. The poor things are quite stricken."

Lord Finlington sighed in response. "Yes, I know. Well, darlings, I'm sure you're thinking what I'm thinking—what to tell your employer when you go back empty-handed, eh?"

Nell had not made it that far, but now that the viscount brought it up, she was startled into worry. What would they say to Jack?

"I don't suppose you could just give it to us, sir?" Pip said, with a sly grin. It was, Nell recognized, the same smile he used when he was distracting marks.

"Oh, good heavens," Lord Finlington said, casting a hand over his face dramatically. "The man has dimples, Charlie." He peeked at Pip from between his fingers and then added, over his shoulder, "Two, Charlie! Two dimples! One on each cheek!"

Mr. Kentworthy threw his head back and laughed at his friend's antics.

The viscount dropped his hand from his face and flapped it at Pip. "Oh, put them away, dear, do. Before you hurt somebody. Namely me. I have far too delicate a constitution." Pip schooled his features as the viscount requested and the gentleman sighed in relief. "No, my beautiful young friend, I cannot just give it to you. Although you are about the only person in the world who might tempt me."

Pip gave him a small smile, looking wholly unrepentant in his attempt.

"If you don't mind my asking, sir," Nell said. "What would you recommend we say to our employer?"

"Does she always get down to cases like this, Pip darling?"

Pip nodded.

"I thought as much. Of course I don't mind you asking, my sweet. I know precisely what you should say to your employer: tell him to meet me at the Fox & Thistle tomorrow night at ten. Oh, and if you two are free, I would be delighted to see you. Always enjoy running into old friends, you know. And introductions are so much easier if one has a mutual acquaintance."

"You want him to meet you at a pub?" Nell repeated, not quite believing the instructions. "And you want us to be there?"

"Yes, yes. Can you make it, dears? I know it is very last-minute, which is unpardonably gauche. But needs must, you know."

"Yes, we'll be there," Nell said, a little stunned.

"Wonderful," Lord Finlington said. He hopped off the desk. "Well, this has been an absolute dream, darlings. But some of us do need our beauty rest, even if you two are utterly gorgeous just the way you are. Come along."

They followed Lord Finlington out of the room. He walked them to the front door and then waved them outside, chattering about how he simply couldn't wait to see them again.

Nell and Pip found themselves standing alone on the viscount's stoop, thoroughly bemused.

"Good Lord," Nell said after the door clicked close behind them. "I've never met anyone like him in my whole life."

"I can't imagine there is anyone else like him," Pip muttered, looking at the door.

She sighed. "Well, come on. Let's get Tom and go tell Jack."

CHAPTER 6

Tom, as it turned out, was nowhere to be found. They surmised that he had seen the lights in the room and ran off when they didn't come back out. Nell couldn't blame him.

They made their way to the tavern, feeling jumpy and bewildered from the strange experience. When they finally reached it, Jack was sitting hunched over an ale, looking more dejected than Nell had ever seen him. As soon as they walked in, he hurried forward to give Pip a crushing hug. He wrapped an arm around Nell as well and led them both to the table, yelling for drinks.

He pulled Pip onto his lap, cradling Pip's head against his shoulder. "Tom came back alone," he said into Pip's hair. "I thought I'd lost you, boy."

"I'm here, Jack," Pip said, sounding muffled. "No need to fuss."

Ignoring him, Jack continued to hold Pip tightly, stroking through his curls with a shaky hand. "What happened?" he asked at last.

Nell took a deep breath. "He's a strong spellcaster, Jack. I...I wasn't prepared for him. He caught us. Caught us as soon as we got into the house, actually."

"How did you get away?"

"He let us go."

Jack's grip on Pip tightened. "Were you followed?"

"No. But he wanted us to tell you to meet him tomorrow night."

"At the Fox & Thistle," Pip murmured into Jack's collar. "At ten."

Jack released his hold on Pip and kissed him hard. "Don't ever scare me like that again," he said, in a harsher tone than Nell had ever heard him use. He was clearly more frightened by their delay than she had expected. He pulled Pip's head back to his shoulder, holding him as if he were a small child, rather than a young man. It seemed as if he thought he could protect Pip from imagined harms by holding him as close as possible.

"Are you going to meet with him?" she asked.

"It could be a trap," he said.

"It could be," Nell agreed. "But I doubt it. He could have turned us in tonight and didn't."

"Maybe he wanted to use you to get to me."

"He doesn't even know who you are," she retorted. "He seemed more interested in who hired you."

Jack arched an eyebrow. "Interesting. I suppose I'll go, if only because I'm curious."

"He wants us to go too," Pip added.

Jack frowned at that. "No. It was a mistake to send you two in the first place. I overestimated your magic ability."

"I'm sorry," she said. "I thought I could do it."

He sighed. "I know," he said. "I didn't realize how close I might come to losing you."

Nell was fairly certain he wasn't talking about her. "I think we should be there," she said.

"Out of the question."

"He wanted us to introduce you," she said.

Jack scoffed. "Of course that's what he'd say."

"I don't think he was being dishonest," Pip said. "He isn't the type."

Jack rolled his eyes and didn't respond.

"He'll be more at ease, I think, if we're there," Pip persisted.

Jack huffed and kissed Pip on the forehead. "I'll think about it."

In the end, Jack relented. Nell suspected that Pip had wheedled his lover once he had him alone. At ten o'clock the following evening, the three of them sat together at the Fox & Thistle, waiting for Lord Finlington.

The viscount arrived looking polished, but in a less flashy way than he had at home. He took a seat next to Nell and pronounced himself delighted to meet Jack.

"My word," he said. "What do they put in the water on your side of London? Such a strapping specimen. Are all the men in your neighborhood as delectable as these two, Nell dear?"

"I'm not sure I'm the right person to ask," Nell replied.

Pip snorted.

Jack slid his arm up Pip's back to cup the back of his neck. He started to stroke Pip's neck in his usual way. "How kind of you to say so, m'lord."

Pip hunched slightly under Jack's touch.

"Well, I've always had a weakness for pretty eyes and dimpled cheeks," the viscount said. His eyes were narrowed but otherwise his expression and tone were light.

Jack glanced at Pip and ran his hand through Pip's hair. "Is that so?" His hand slid back down to continue stroking Pip's neck. "Is that what you wanted to talk to me about?"

"You don't waste time, do you?" Lord Finlington said. "Excellent. Well, I do appreciate efficiency. And thank you for coming on such short notice. The matter I wanted to discuss is some dreadful curiosity on my part in how you came to know of my little possession."

"I'm afraid I can't tell you that."

The viscount smiled, unperturbed. "Of course, silly of me. But perhaps you'd be so kind as to tell me how much our astute friend paid you to rob me."

Jack blinked, surprised. "Thirty pounds," he said.

The viscount's smile widened. "A paltry sum, I do hate to tell you. However, I wonder if I might induce you to give up the endeavor."

"What do you mean?"

"I will pay you fifty pounds to not attempt to rob me again."

Jack looked floored by the offer.

"It is not that I fear you actually being successful," Lord Finlington went on. "But it is a bit of a nuisance. I would rest more easily at night if I trusted you to have the situation in hand. I should so hate having to bring the constabulary into the affair. Much tidier to settle between friends, don't you agree?"

"I like the way you think, your lordship."

"Wonderful." The viscount pulled a purse out of his waistcoat and placed it in front of Jack.

Jack looked consideringly at the viscount, then dug into his own pocket and pulled out a few coins. He passed them to Nell. "Go fetch us a round, will you?"

She did as requested. By the time she returned to the table, the viscount was gone, Pip looked stricken, and Jack looked smug. They didn't speak while they drank their ale, although Jack interrupted his own drinking to nuzzle against Pip's cheek and occasionally plant little kisses from Pip's temple to his jaw. Afterward, Nell walked out of the pub alone and Jack, with an arm slung around Pip's shoulders, walked them both to his place.

She never did find out what passed between the three men while she was at the bar. She wondered if Lord Finlington had flirted in a way that went too far. Jack was awfully protective of Pip. She said as much to Patience that night, puzzling over the matter out loud.

Patience had sighed and squinted at the mending she was doing. "You know you could ask Pip if you're so curious about it."

"I'm not sure he'd appreciate that."

Patience raised an eyebrow. "Then he probably wouldn't appreciate you speculating about it to me, now would he?"

Nell picked up a stocking from the pile next to her friend. "Probably not. But then Pip barely talks to me anymore."

"He always was quiet, you know."

"Not to me." She twisted the stocking in her hand. "He's always been able to talk to me. Any time he was in trouble, I always got him out of it. I know he has Jack now, so he doesn't need me like he used to. But still, I wish he'd trust me a bit more."

Patience glanced up at her, gently pried the stocking out of her hands, and tossed it back on the pile. "He's older than you. Maybe he doesn't want to burden you with the task of always looking after him."

"It's not a burden. I looked out for him because I wanted to and...and he needed it."

Patience tilted her head. "Well, we all have to grow up eventually, Nelly," she said. "Maybe Pip's decided that part of growing up means not depending on you anymore."

Nell sighed and leaned on her hand. "I suppose you're right. Still hurts, though."

Patience reached over and squeezed her hand. "I know. I'm sorry." Then she returned to the mending.

Nell frowned at the pile. "Do you really have to do all of that tonight?"

"Jack managed to get me working the day shift. Night's the best time for me to do these things."

"Yes, but does it have to be right now?"

Patience raised an eyebrow again. "Can you think of a better time?"

"I just…" Nell gestured vaguely. "I only see Pip when I'm working. And almost every time I see you, you're…busy doing something or other. It's the mending tonight. Last time I stopped by, you were making soup, of all things—"

"And why shouldn't I make soup?"

"I don't have anything against soup. I just want to do the things we used to do."

Patience pursed her lips and focused on her mending. "Don't I always make room for you in my bed when you come by?"

"I don't mean that. Not that I don't enjoy that, of course, but I like having you as a friend too."

"We're friends now, aren't we?" Patience said in a terse voice.

"Yes, but Pip's always busy with Jack and you're always busy with…"

Patience gave her a hard look. "With…what, Nell? My children? My family? Did you forget that I have one of those?"

Nell didn't like the idea that unspoken was the notion that *she* didn't have a family. She pushed past that troubling thought and said, "Of course I didn't. But do you really have to spend every night at home? Why don't we go to the tavern or the market? We could share a loaf of sweet bread." She leaned forward and nuzzled Patience's cheek. "I know you have a weakness for those."

Patience turned and planted a kiss on Nell's mouth before turning back to her work. "You only know that because of the time I nabbed a loaf instead of a purse. And you know I can't just leave my children home alone while I gad about town. I already told you that. If you want to see me, it has to be at home, or not at all."

Nell almost teased her friend for not being any fun, but

thought better of it. There was a pinched look to Patience's expression that made her wary of pursuing the topic further. Instead she tilted her face to nibble at the other woman's neck. "Perhaps you need a break from all the mending?" she said in a sweet tone.

Patience let out a breathy laugh. "Oh, all right, you charmer. Help me clear these things off the bed."

Soon all thoughts of Patience's pinched expression, her own lack of family, the fear that she was losing two of her friends, and the whole matter of the viscount's sudden departure were all out of Nell's head.

As she strode from Patience's door later that night, she began to think about her present situation. Jack would likely still give her the promised five pounds. If she took smaller cuts from her takes this week, she would have enough to pay off her debt. Perhaps the solution to her friends no longer needing her was to no longer need them. Jack didn't seem interested in her magical abilities anymore. It pained her to think of leaving Pip behind, but she had left him behind before. She liked to think looking after Pip was where she belonged, but he kept pushing her away. Perhaps Patience was right after all and it was time for them both to grow up. She went to her own bed and pondered the matter.

By the time Pip came by to collect her for work, she had made up her mind. She did not tell Pip of the plans she had brewing, but she believed Jack suspected what she was up to when she started taking smaller cuts. He kept giving her shrewd looks. Within the week, she had paid off her debt to Jack, including her money for rent.

The next day, Nell made her way back to Lord Finlington's grand home, and knocked on the door.

A tall footman who hadn't been there the night of the burglary opened the door and raised his eyebrows imperiously. "Yes?"

"I wish to speak to Lord Finlington, please."

The imperious eyebrows slanted downward. "Who may I say is calling?"

"The name's Nell."

The footman closed the door. A moment later, he opened it again and stepped aside for her to come in. Wordlessly, the footman led her back to the viscount's study.

"Nell, you dear girl! To what do I owe the pleasure?" Lord Finlington said as he directed her to one of the wingback chairs. He perched on the edge of the desk, much as he had the other night.

Nell took a steadying breath, her hands clenched together. "I was wondering if I might ask you to teach me."

He cocked his head, waiting for her to continue.

"In magic," she said. "I want to learn more magic. I don't know how much you'd charge, but I have some money. And I can work for it. That is, I can work for you in exchange for the lessons."

"What a charming notion," he replied. "But I am surprised, m'dear. You seem to have a job already."

"I don't want to be a thief," she said. "I left Jack's employment years ago. I've been doing honest work wherever I could get it, at shops and the like."

"Ah, how you met dear Charlie, I take it?"

"Yes," she said. "That was the reason I was back with Jack, you see. The whole mess with Mr. Kentworthy. I sort of owed Jack for stealing from him, considering how much they would have gotten off of Mr. Kentworthy. I've been working it off. The burglary was supposed to clear my debt with him."

"And has it?"

She nodded. "I know I'm good at thieving, but it's not what I want. And working odd-jobs is barely enough to live on." She paused, wondering how forthright she should be.

"Yes?" he prompted gently.

"I'm hoping that if I can learn magic, I can find a way to get out of that whole business. Find a better life for myself."

He didn't say anything for a few moments, looking at her consideringly and kicking one foot in an idle way. "I daresay it might suit," he said at last. "Have you any notion what you might do once you learn enough?"

She shook her head. "But I've heard some places keep spellcasters on staff."

"Where did you learn magic?"

"I've watched the street magicians and Mr. Smelting."

He raised an eyebrow. "My word, darling. Self-taught? Very impressive. I suppose Pip learned it the same way?"

She frowned. "Pip? He doesn't—"

He waved a hand airily. "The lock, m'dear. Only a person with an innate magical ability could have picked it. Not to mention he sensed one of the traps I had laid. Even resisted it. Most remarkable," he muttered, as if to himself. "Is Pip aware of this plan of yours? Do you think he'd be interested in joining you?"

"No, I don't think he would." she said. "When I left Jack's employment before, I sort of thought Pip would come with me. But he didn't. And now…" She took a breath. "Now, I don't think he'd leave if I asked him. I'm almost certain of it."

"Your friend Jack has quite a hold on him, I gather."

"Well, they are together. I'm pretty sure Jack's teaching Pip more of what he does so Pip can take over someday."

"Somehow, I don't think retirement is weighing heavily on that Jack fellow's mind," the viscount remarked drily, examining his fingernails. "But you'll forgive me for saying so, dear. You know the man so much better than I do. Well, as I said the other night, I do hate to see good talent go to waste. So I shall accept you as a pupil. However, there will be some conditions."

Nell's heart leapt and she sat up straight. "Yes?"

"You will understand, I hope, that I am reluctant to trust anyone who remains in your friend Jack's social sphere."

She frowned. "What do you mean?"

"I mean that even if you are no longer working for him, you will likely still be around him quite often, simply because you spend a great deal of time with Pip. And if what you say is true, and Pip is learning to follow in Jack's footsteps, I'm not sure it wise for you to stay in that environment at all. So, I will accept you as a pupil and you may repay me for the education by working as my assistant on two conditions. First, you will live with me while you are learning."

"Live here?"

"Yes, and don't worry, darling. You will be perfectly safe. Even if I was inclined in your direction, I assure you I'm a gentleman."

She considered this a moment. "What's the second condition?"

He smiled. "You will tell Pip about your plan, all of it. You will tell him that you are coming to live with me, that you will be learning magic, that you will be working as my assistant, and that you hope to find a good enough job to get you out of your current situation."

She gaped. "Why?"

Lord Finlington's look softened. "Because the poor young man deserves to make his own choices for a change. He must understand what you are working toward and make up his own mind if he wants the same thing that you do. When you leave this time, he will have the choice to leave with you."

"I don't think he'll come along. But I'll certainly ask him if you'd like."

He hopped off the desk. "Excellent. I wish everyone in London were as decisive as you, m'dear. I can't abide dithering."

Nell tossed and turned all night, trying to think of how to broach the subject with Pip and anticipating what he would say. She tried to imagine Pip leaving Jack and she found she couldn't picture it. Then again, Viscount Finlinton had mentioned that Pip had magical talents as well. She remembered the time Pip had asked her to teach him magic. Perhaps if he did agree to join her, it would mean that she had been right: looking after Pip was where she belonged.

The next morning, she was ready. She had already paid Jack what she owed him, and she was confident he wouldn't be broken up by her departure, particularly since her magical talents had not served his purpose. When Pip came by to meet her for work, she had already packed a knapsack of her meager belongings, and was sitting on her mattress, eager to go.

Pip took in her knapsack and excitement in one glance. He didn't seem surprised, only weary. "Moving? You know you'll blow through that five pounds if you spend it all on a better room."

"Pip, Lord Finlington's going to teach me magic."

Pip paused in the act of sitting down. "Oh."

"He's taking me on as his assistant in exchange for the lessons."

He sat down with a thump and tucked his feet under himself. "That's nice of him."

"I'm moving in with him."

Pip did seem surprised at that. He glanced up at her. "Are you sure that's wise?"

"I don't think he'll try anything."

"You don't know that."

She didn't respond.

Pip scrubbed a hand over his face. "You're right. He's not the type."

She took a deep breath. "Come with me, Pip."

He froze.

"I won't have to leave you behind this time. You can come with me. He'll teach us both. He said you have potential too. We can get out of this place. Get out of this life."

Pip didn't say anything for a long moment. He looked down and picked at a thread on his mattress blanket.

"For goodness' sake, say something," Nell said, exasperated. "Don't you want to come with me?"

"It's not that," he said, sighing. "I'm...I'm not like you, you know. I never planned for other possibilities. I'm good at what I do and I...I'm not one to reach for what isn't meant for me. I'm glad for you, Nelly. I really am. You know I've always wanted the best for you. Jack's always said you've got ambitions. He's right. You're better than this life. You're meant for greatness, I've always believed that."

She got up and sat next to him, wrapping an arm around his shoulder. "So are you, Pip."

He leaned his head on her shoulder. "Did you tell Jack you were leaving?"

"I paid off my debt. I didn't think I owed him any more of an explanation, you know?"

He nodded. "Probably right."

"You're sure you don't want to chance it with me?"

He sighed. "I can't forever be hiding behind you for protection, Nelly. I'll muddle along well enough. You'd better go. You wouldn't want to keep his lordship waiting. And I need to go tell Jack in case he doesn't want me working alone today."

She squeezed his shoulder. "At least I know he'll take proper care of you. I'll rest easy knowing you've got someone else who loves you and is looking after you at last."

He didn't respond and pulled away from her embrace. She figured that was her cue to go. She picked up her knapsack off her mattress and stood.

He reached up and grabbed her wrist. "You're going to be brilliant, Nelly," he said, earnest. Then he gave her a small grin. "Just don't get so grand that you forget about me."

She sat back down and pulled him into a tight hug. "I would never."

CHAPTER 7

LORD FINLINGTON DID NOT SEEM surprised to see her arrive alone.

"He didn't want to come," she said simply.

The viscount did not probe further, welcoming her with delight.

Thus, Nell embarked on a thrilling new part of her life.

She was led upstairs to a lovely little room, which was all her own and included a huge, comfortable bed. The large windows looked out on Berkeley Square. Nell was stunned for a moment, realizing that for once in her life, she was situated among the wealthy people of London. It was an exhilarating thought. It was a new beginning. She was finally walking away from everything she had known, the way of life that had kept her in poverty, and she was moving up.

As she stood at the window, reveling in the thought, a bath was brought up and the maids quickly filled it with water. Nell watched, intrigued, as one of the maids set up a couple of spells beside the tub.

"What's that for?" she asked.

The maid looked up in surprise. "This, miss? It's just a standard heating spell."

Nell looked on in amazement as the maid cast the spell; it

was unlike any other she'd seen before. "Why did you do all that…with the chalk and everything?"

The maid blinked. "It's a common spell, miss. I don't do Motion work. A little too advanced for me."

Motion work? Was that what Nell had taught herself? She liked the idea that she had learned something advanced.

Another maid instructed Nell to take off her clothes and get into the tub. She sank into the hot water and felt immediately relaxed. She washed herself, feeling as if she was truly in the lap of luxury. Her skin wasn't the only thing being scrubbed clean; her whole life was being transformed. The dingy bathwater served as visible proof of what she was leaving behind.

After the bath, she learned that the viscount had ordered dresses for her.

"His lordship said you may not want someone dressing you every day," the maid went on. "So these are ones you can do yourself." She indicated ones with ties up the front. "These are a little fancier, and you'll need one of us to help you."

Feeling pampered, Nell chose one of the fancier dresses. The maid put her hair into a simple updo. Then Nell stood in front of a tall looking glass and examined her reflection. It was strange, seeing herself in something so fine. She skimmed her fingers over the fabric, enjoying the softness of the material. The idea of such grand clothing being truly hers made her giddy. This new stage in life was temporary, but it didn't mean she couldn't enjoy it while it lasted.

She stood for a long moment, lost in thought. This was not her destination, she reminded herself. She was here to learn and to work, and then she would move on to a new job and a new life. She figured it was safe to assume that she would have to pay the viscount for all of the clothes, but she suspected he would be kind about it. He was so generous, he probably wouldn't even be bothered if she had to continue paying him after she found new work.

She went downstairs and found the viscount in his study, clearly unconcerned about the wait. He took her on a tour of the townhouse, telling her to make herself at home. He insisted she address him as Bertie, which delighted her, for she enjoyed the sensation of having such a great man as a friend.

Bertie informed her that prior to magical lessons, she must first learn to read, an addition to the curriculum that Nell had not anticipated. She spent the first month of her stay learning letters and reading primers. Although she was disappointed at first not to jump straight into magic, she couldn't deny that it was empowering to learn how to read. Bertie had a magnificent library, with more books than she had ever seen in one place. It thrilled her to think someday she would be able to read them all. She wanted to get to magic sooner rather than later, so she applied herself to the task of learning to read with her usual diligence. She turned out to be a quick study, and she basked in the glow of Bertie's subsequent praise of her speedy progress.

After she had been with Bertie for a full month, he started teaching her magic. He began with magic theory, which turned out to be far more complicated than she had anticipated.

"Can't I just learn how to cast things like I always do?" she asked.

Bertie considered this question. "I'm afraid you may have to unlearn a great deal of what you already know, m'dear. And I suspect you will learn best by understanding theories first. However, I may be mistaken. So if you want to know the practical side of magic first—"

"I do."

He tilted his head. "Very well, darling."

Nell had hoped for more magic like what she had seen on the streets. But Bertie insisted that the basics must be learned first. Basic spellwork was more complex and involved than what she had been doing. There were multiple ingredients and everything had to be laid out on the floor just so and paired with sigils and incantations. Nell found herself asking a great many questions: "What does this sigil *mean*, though?" "Why use a feather?" "Is the circle really necessary?"

Bertie answered all of her questions ("It means that the magic will be used to make items levitate, darling." "The feather has the right Constitutional Properties for floating, you see." "The circle dictates what is included in the spell. Otherwise, the magic might try to make everything float. Dashed nuisance trying to fix that.").

But after a week of magical training, he sat her down and said, "Darling, I feel that a theory-based learning plan might work best for you after all."

Nell slumped. "But I want to *do* magic."

He smiled. "You're frightfully clever, m'dear. I'm sure you'll pick up the theory in no time at all, and will be doing magic with flair in a matter of months. But it may be less frustrating for you if you understand the reasons behind it before you jump into the practical end of things."

She glanced at the wobbly sigil she had chalked into the floor. She did want to know what the symbols meant. She sighed. "Oh, all right."

"Would it help if I started training you as my assistant?"

She had been wondering about that, worrying a bit that her debt was building up while she was staying at his house for free and learning to read. She agreed enthusiastically.

The next day, he started training her. Being Bertie's assistant turned out to mean a great deal of assorted duties. Some of them were familiar to her—like cleaning up after his experiments and spell work. She was surprised to discover that sometimes Bertie made just as much of a mess as Mr. Smelting. Bertie laughed when she commented on it and told her that magic is a messy sort of business. Cleaning up after a spell could be as simple as putting away the materials and scrubbing up the sigils chalked into the workspace, or it could be as involved as setting the entire room to rights. Sometimes Bertie needed so much space for a spell that he would ask her to help him move the furniture and roll up the carpet. It could be an arduous process. Nell had always been comfortable with physical work, so she applied herself to these tasks with enthusiasm.

Then, Nell's theory lessons began.

"Now, the first thing you must learn is Sandellini's Theory of Constitutional Properties." Bertie smiled at her perplexed expression. "This is really just a fancy way of saying that everything, manmade or natural, has a sort of *personality* to it, if you will. For instance, the traditional levitation spell utilizes a feather. This is because the Constitutional Properties of a feather, the personality or the nature of it, is that it is practically weightless. Thus, you transpose those properties from the feather into the magic, causing whatever it is you are casting it on to adopt those properties. Do you see?"

She nodded and sat up straighter.

"The good thing about this theory is that you can personalize spells based on what you have at hand or what you prefer to use, so long as they have the same Constitutional Properties of the item in the original spell. The bad is there is no other way to learn the properties of every possible magical ingredient other than memorizing the most commonly used ones.

"This," he continued, pushing a book forward, "is the list of commonly used ingredients and materials, the ones found in traditional spells. You should know that some of the traditional materials are not the strongest or the best. This is why in modern spellcasting, the list gets even longer and is practically endless. We will stick with the traditional ones first, but it is still quite a lengthy list. I would like you to memorize it before you begin any spellwork."

As she had only just learned to read, working through the

list was slow-going. She was grateful when Bertie left her to it and she muddled through the long list alone.

Another component to living with Bertie that Nell did not anticipate was the gentleman's social calendar. After her first month, she found that he was often busy with different social obligations. He would leave in the evening and not come back until early morning. He would stroll out, finely dressed, for dinner parties or the opera. Every morning, he would go out riding in the park. And every now and again, when he was assured that she had plenty of work to keep her busy, he would leave in the middle of the day.

Sometimes his social calendar would involve Nell, in that people came to his home for dinner or tea and he would invite Nell to join. In this way, she was reacquainted with Mr. Kentworthy (who asked her to call him Charles), and met his fiancé, a shy and quiet gentleman named Mr. Hartford, and Mr. Hartford's sister, a beautiful and charming young lady.

At first, Nell was not particularly fond of either of the Hartford siblings. Mr. Hartford was too timid to keep up an interesting conversation. When she met Miss Hartford, Bertie was so enthusiastic in his praise of the young lady's magical talent, Nell took an instant dislike for the woman she considered her rival. But that dislike did not last very long. Miss Hartford seemed determined to befriend her. When she clasped Nell's hand and said how thrilled she was to meet another lady who loved magic and could appreciate how marvelous it was, Nell decided friendship was a good sight more comfortable than competition. The fact that she was also a beautiful creature with copper-colored hair did much to endear her.

While Bertie's social circle seemed quite large, Nell only met the three individuals who visited most. Bertie explained that he did not want to overwhelm her with too many introductions. But as he appeared to be a highly social person, the more Nell seemed able to study on her own, the more Bertie left her to study in privacy while he gadded about with various acquaintances. Nell didn't mind; she appreciated his trust in her to study as she ought and not to rob him.

She was surprised, however, when he began inviting her on some of his outings. The first place he took her to was a fine restaurant, with white tablecloths, gleaming silverware, and crystal glasses. Nell initially considered this simply a treat and she reveled in the experience. However, as they waited for their meal, Bertie began directing her attention to some of the staff members standing around the room.

"There," he said, pointing, "is a spellcaster. You can tell because of the little apron he is wearing. Those are to hold his ingredients and tools. Keep an eye on that one, darling. And tell me what you can observe about his work."

Intrigued, Nell did as instructed. She saw the spellcaster cast something at the punch bowl ("refreshing the cooling spell," Bertie explained), and would sometimes trail behind a server when a tray was being carried ("no doubt there is a spell to keep it from being too heavy, you see"), and would generally drift around the room and work on spells that Nell hadn't even realized were set up along the wall ("Do you notice how cool and airy the room is, m'dear? Cooling spells are everywhere"). She had known for a long time that she wished to find work in magic, but actually seeing people who did it amazed her.

After dinner, Bertie prodded her with questions. He wanted to know what she had observed, what confused her, what intrigued her, and what excited her.

"It was wonderful to see spellcasters in action," she said. "I've never known what they actually do."

He smiled. "I'm delighted to hear it, darling. Now, a few things to keep in mind. We went to dinner, I regret to say, at an unfashionable time. Did you notice how few people were at the tables? I wanted you to have a better view of the staff, you see. Ordinarily, there would be less standing around and more of a constant rotation between spells. One spellcaster might be assigned to simply walk the room and check the cooling spells, another might be directed to assist with the heavy trays, another might check the spells around the food and drinks. That sort of thing. So keep that in mind when considering your future occupation."

"Thank you, Bertie."

"Don't mention it, my sweet. That was only our first place of observation. I have a few others in mind. I want you to have a better idea of your options. You may like none of what I can show you, but it will at least give you a good sense of what your prospects are."

A few days later, Nell was surprised by a visitor. Miss Hartford strolled into the library where Nell was still struggling through the list Bertie had given her.

"I hope you don't think me too forward," the lady said after greeting her. "But I thought it would be nice to join you for tea."

Nell had never had someone visit her for tea, so she wasn't entirely sure of the protocols in such a situation. She slid a slip of paper into her book to mark her place and turned to thank Miss Hartford for visiting.

"Oh dear," the lady said. "Am I interrupting your reading?"

Nell shrugged. "Just studying. It's all right."

"What are you studying?"

"Constitutional Properties."

"Oh! Is Bertie making you memorize them? That's how I had to start too. It's such a long list!"

Nell smiled. "I'm glad to hear you say that. I thought it was just me."

"Not at all!" Miss Hartford gave her a thoughtful look. "Would you like some help? I don't mean to presume, of course. My brother Gavin and I had to memorize the list when we were children. I have several tricks for remembering that I can show you."

Nell didn't hesitate long before agreeing to Miss Hartford's offer.

Thus, Miss Hartford's teatime visit turned into another lesson, of sorts. True to her word, the lady had several tricks for memorizing some of the properties in a way that stuck in Nell's head. Miss Hartford returned several days in a row to continue to help. Nell had the list memorized by the end of the week.

She thanked Miss Hartford as they finally closed the book.

Miss Hartford smiled. "Happy to help, Miss Birks. Quite frankly, I love meeting people who are as interested in magic as I am. You are very clever, so it was no hardship helping you."

"Magic isn't usually available to people like me," Nell admitted.

"Bertie says you have a remarkable natural talent."

Nell grinned at the praise. "I want to be a spellcaster. I'm hoping after I learn everything I can from Bertie, I can find a good job somewhere."

Miss Hartford clapped her hands. "How thrilling! I'm sure I would love to do magic for a living."

"Really?" Nell said, surprised. "I would have thought you'd want to marry someone grand."

Miss Hartford sighed. "Yes, I know. It's what I'm supposed to want. Charles is trying to help me find a husband."

Nell studied her for a moment. "You don't want to be married?"

The lady gave a delicate shrug. "I'm terribly romantic, so I would adore falling in love and getting married but…" She hesitated for a moment and then scooted closer to Nell on the sofa, as if she were about to impart a great secret. "I really think I'd prefer to be a spellmaster," she said in a low voice.

"It would be enjoyable and challenging and I would just adore it."

"Why don't you?" Nell thought the answer seemed obvious. Miss Hartford was clearly wealthy and elegant. Couldn't she get whatever she wanted?

Miss Hartford shook her head. "It's technically frowned upon in my position. I have a younger brother, and if I went to work, it might make it too difficult for him to find a spouse. I might be willing to risk it, but you see, I'm a nextborn, so I don't have very much by way of money or stability. It would likely be far outside my resources to run a shop. So it is impossible financially as well as socially. And I can't imagine any man would support a wife in trade."

"That is unfortunate," Nell said. She'd never considered the possibility of being too high on the social ladder to do what one wanted. But she knew how hard it was to have dreams that were just out of reach.

"Ah well," Miss Hartford said with a sad smile. "I'm very fortunate, so it is selfish to complain too much. But it is kind of you to be sympathetic."

"What are friends for?" Nell said, returning the smile.

Miss Hartford clasped her hand gratefully.

Later, Nell thought about her new and budding friendship. It was nice to have a new friend, but as she lay in bed, she found herself missing her other friends, the ones she'd left behind. Thoughts of Pip still made her feel anxious in a way she couldn't quite understand. But thinking of Patience made her feel lonely; she missed Patience's touch, her laugh, her kisses.

No sooner had she gotten into bed, she decided to get back out of it. She put on a simple dress, threw on a dark coat, and slipped out of the dark and quiet townhouse. She expected more interruptions getting to Patience's door, but she only got accosted once or twice, and easily maneuvered out of the encounters. Her steps were quick, but the walk was long, so by the time she reached Patience's door, she was a little out of breath.

Patience opened the door and her eyes widened. "Well, blow me down with a feather," she said succinctly.

"You busy tonight?"

Patience was still staring at her with unabashed shock. "And where were you? Vauxhall Gardens? Buckingham Palace?"

Nell rolled her eyes. "Oh, come off it, do. It's only me. I thought we could go for a walk by the river or something, like we used to."

Patience frowned. "I can't, Nelly. You know I can't."

"Please?" Nell pleaded. "I miss you."

"I miss you too, but I can't—"

"Just for one night?" She leaned forward and pressed a kiss to her friend's mouth. "You can step away for just one night, can't you?"

Patience's eyes narrowed. "Why must you always do this?"

Nell pulled back, surprised. "What do you mean?"

"I keep telling you I can't do that sort of thing anymore. I can't go gadding off to the river or out for a pint or a walk around the market. Not anymore."

"You can't have fun anymore, is that what you're saying?"

Patience let out a frustrated huff. "And staying the night isn't fun enough for you, is it?"

"Of course it is, but you're always having to *do* things."

"This is my life. Why can't you understand?"

"Yes, I know. Your *family* and everything," Nell said, unable to keep the bitterness out of her voice.

Patience looked pained.

Nell sighed. "What would you have me do then?"

"I want...I want you to understand that this is my life now. You can be a part of it, if you'd like. But I can't change it just for you. I can't go out at night anymore. I can't wander around during the day either because I've got my work. But...but you can come over any night you like. I have some extra soup—although it doesn't look like you need any food from me, if those fancy clothes are anything to go by. You can sit with me while I do the mending. The girls are both in bed already. We could talk in my room? I just...I like your company. But I can't do what we used to do."

Nell swallowed. What Patience was describing sounded an awful lot like marriage and that was far from Nell's plans. She stood silently for a long moment, trying to think of what to say. All she could manage was a quiet, "Oh."

Patience sniffed. "It isn't fair, you know."

"What?"

Patience gestured at her in a vague sort of way. "You—you go and grow up and change and lead whatever life you want. And you expect everyone else—you expect *me* to just...stay the same forever?"

"I do not—"

"I'm not who I used to be. Neither is Pip. But neither are you. How is that you can take a step up in life but when I—"

"This is hardly the same thing."

Hurt flashed across Patience's face. "I can't do this anymore," she said, leaning against the door frame. She looked tired.

"Can't do what?" Nell said, alarmed.

Patience scrubbed a hand over her face. "This...whatever this is. I can't keep defending myself to you. If you can't accept me as I am now then...then I think that's...it."

"I can't be what you want me to be," Nell said.

"You're not even going to try?"

Nell tried to imagine herself being married and quickly shut the thought down. "I can't. And I don't think it's fair for you to ask me."

Patience let out a humorless huff. "That's it then."

Nell swallowed, afraid to say the next words. "I guess it's...goodbye?"

"Yeah," Patience said sadly. "I guess it is. Take care of yourself, Nelly."

"You too, Patience."

The door was closed softly in her face. She trudged back home, her mood somber. It was clear that Pip was pushing her away, but she had hoped Patience would still be part of her life. Would she have to let go of all of her past friends to find out where she belonged? When she walked back into Bertie's house, she was surprised to find him waiting for her.

He looked relieved to see her. "Everything all right, m'dear?"

She shrugged, a little embarrassed to explain her trip to him. "Just visiting a friend."

"Pip?"

"No," she said. "Another friend. A...different sort of friend."

"Ah," he said in a tone that suggested understanding and also, confusingly, disappointment. "Did you have a pleasant time?"

"Not really," she admitted. "It would appear I'm not welcome there anymore."

"I'm sorry, darling," he said, wrapping an arm around her shoulders and leading her up the stairs. "Would you like a glass of wine or something? To cushion the blow a bit?"

She chuckled. "No, that's all right. Thank you all the same."

"You can sleep late tomorrow if you'd like. We can go over the lessons I had planned another day."

"We're supposed to do lessons?" she said, pausing mid-step.

"Well, you did finish memorizing that list. I promised you more theory after that."

"Please don't push the lessons back," she pleaded. "That will definitely make up for tonight."

He laughed. "Very good, darling."

Nell was still feeling discouraged as she returned to bed. She held onto the thought that even if she had to leave Pip and Patience behind, maybe she could find her place with her new friends, Bertie, Charles, and Miss Hartford.

CHAPTER 8

TRUE TO HIS WORD, the next day Bertie taught Nell about Norton's Theorem of Magical Absorbance, which turned out to be a convoluted way of saying that everything, living or inanimate, natural or manmade, had the capacity to be impacted by magic. Bertie explained the theory, the history, and how it was applied practically. He then taught her a spell that exemplified this theorem so she could see it in context. It was a levitation spell, but he demonstrated several times with a range of focuses: a feather, a metal spoon, and even had her stand in the circle to be levitated. Afterwards, they discussed how each of the focuses had reacted (they had all levitated as they had been directed to do). When he was confident she understood the spell, he told her to practice on her own until she had it mastered.

Before she had the spell mastered, Bertie took her to another place to see spellcaster work, which turned out to be Almack's. It was during the day, which Bertie explained apologetically was the only time he could get her into the ballroom.

"They are frightfully particular, I'm afraid," he said. "Even wealthy and titled guests have to be vouched for to be welcome. However, I have been in contact with the head of magical staff. She told me to bring you to a side entrance. Ah, here we are."

He opened a small door towards the back of the building and ushered her in.

They were met by a dour woman who looked over Nell disapprovingly, but was very respectful to Bertie.

"Miss Locke, this is my student and assistant," Bertie said. "Miss Nell Birks. She is only just beginning her official magical education, but she shows a great deal of promise. I should like to show her what sort of careers spellcasters might pursue."

Miss Locke proceeded to take them on a hurried tour through the building. She showed them the kitchens and where the refreshment tables were set up in the ballrooms.

"Here is the set up for a cooling spell, do you see?" Bertie said. "And more along the wall there. These are only the bare bones of the spell, however. Most likely the rest of the spell is set up and activated at the time of events."

"We take pride in our cooling spells here," Miss Locke said. "The rooms get very warm of an evening. Everyone on my staff must be quick on their feet."

Bertie pointed to the chandeliers. "Those are likely lit by magic as well. Is that right, Miss Locke?"

The lady confirmed this, adding that she only entrusted her most senior staff with that responsibility.

They walked through the card rooms, where Nell was shown the set ups for light amplification spells that made the rooms brighter.

When they finally left, Nell felt exhausted by the information and the hurried explanations.

"What do you think, darling?"

"I think I'd prefer the restaurant," she said.

He laughed. "Miss Locke is so very austere, isn't she? I daresay she is difficult to win over. However, I imagine you would learn a great deal working with her. She is one of the most talented spellcasters in London."

Nell considered this. It hadn't occurred to her that her education might continue after she'd left Bertie's employment. She still wasn't keen on the idea of working for the stern woman, but she suspected Bertie had not made the comment lightly, so she resolved to keep the ballroom as a viable option.

The next theory she learned about was Pechard's Hypothesis on Magical Energy, which was a sort of expansion on Norton's theorem, proposing that the reason for magical absorbance was because all things had some amount of magic in them already. She had a harder time wrapping her mind around this one; she didn't understand why more people didn't perform magic, if they all had the capacity to do so. Bertie explained it was a matter of interest and natural ability.

"Everyone can," he explained. "But that doesn't mean everyone can do it well. Not to mention, many do not have the resources to learn, as you are well aware."

Miss Hartford came by for tea again and helped Nell practice the spell assigned for the lesson.

"You really don't have to," Nell said. "I don't want you to do more work than you need to."

"What are friends for?" Miss Hartford said with a grin. "How was Almack's?"

"It was very grand," Nell said. "But I'm not sure I liked Miss Locke."

"Is she in charge of the spellcasting staff?"

Nell nodded. "She was very severe."

"Almack's is a very stuffy sort of place, so that does sound about right."

"Have you been?"

Miss Hartford shook her head. "I want to, though. Being invited to Almack's is something of a status symbol. I'm hoping the Dukex of Molbury procures us vouchers. But I don't want to ask because they've done so much for my brother and I already."

Nell didn't know who the dukex was, but she wasn't sure if she should ask. "Wouldn't that push you closer to marriage?" she said.

"I suppose," she said. "But I do adore dancing. Besides, it's very exciting to see fashionable people."

"I should have thought you'd be considered fashionable," Nell said.

Miss Hartford grinned. "What a lovely thing to say, Miss Birks! I'm very fond of fashion, but in point of fact, I'm from a very small village in the country. So I'm considered more of a country bumpkin than anything else."

Nell didn't try to hide her surprise. "Really?"

"Society is a finicky thing," Miss Hartford said.

"You know you don't need to call me Miss Birks," Nell said after a moment. "My friends call me Nell."

Miss Hartford pulled her into an embrace. "Capital! And do call me Gerry."

Nell adored the fact that her new friends were so informal. She knew they were all above her station, but she had a small hope that even though her time working for Bertie was temporary, she might get to retain these newly made friendships.

Gerry was certainly a very different sort of friend than Patience or Pip had been. But after all, Patience had pointed that Nell was growing up and changing; why couldn't her friendships change too? Even her friendship with Pip, although not as fractured as the one with Patience, felt fragile. She hated the feeling of having left him behind, or having been shoved out of his life.

She had been lonely since her visit to Patience but she liked to think that these new friendships could fill the void that had been left by her past friends. Neither Bertie nor Gerry seemed the type to push her away without warning.

She began to look forward to her visits from Gerry more and more. They talked about marriage, society, Gerry's family, and magic. She learned that Gerry was the third of four children and all of her siblings were brothers. Nell had already met Gavin, who was apparently the secondborn in the family. Gerry explained that even though Gavin was shy and quiet in front of others, he talked much more when he was around people he knew. Nell was surprised to hear that the grave young man was also somewhat sarcastic. Gerry talked about her brother John, who was the oldest and who, apparently, no one in the family got along with. He was the only Hartford sibling who was married; although the family liked his wife even less than they liked him. Her younger brother, Seb, was still at school and something of a trouble-maker. She enjoyed hearing Gerry's observations and comments about each of her brothers and felt a little wistful at the thought of having siblings. Nell found it fascinating how Gerry and Gavin seemed to look after each other; Gerry was just as worried about her brother as he was about her, despite the fact that he was older. It reminded her of her relationship with Pip, who was the closest thing to a sibling she had.

She took in everything Gerry wanted to tell her, forming opinions about all of Gerry's various acquaintances. She tried to think of ways that Gerry could find a career in magic despite the expectation of marriage and hoped that Gerry would get that invitation to Almack's.

One day, Gerry bustled into the library, practically vibrating with excitement. "We're going to Almack's!" She grabbed Nell's hands and whirled them both around. "The dukex got us vouchers! I can't believe it!"

"When?"

Gerry stopped whirling. "In a week! It isn't nearly enough time to have a new dress made, which is a shame. I have one that I haven't worn this Season, so I'm going to see if I can have it altered to be a bit more fashionable." She paused, looking troubled. "I do hope I don't look silly."

"Don't be ridiculous," Nell said. "You're stunning. You'll likely have tons of admirers."

Gerry grinned. "Flatterer."

"I'm sure of it. And you will have to come back the next day and tell me all about it."

"I will." Gerry's grin faltered a bit. "I wish you could come too."

Nell laughed and guided Gerry to a sofa and rang for tea. "That's not for me. I've always known I was meant for more than the life I had, but I don't want ballgowns and fine china."

"What do you want?"

"I want my own bed, I want people to respect me, I want good friends, and I want an honest job where I get to do magic and I make enough money to not be indebted to anyone."

"That's a marvelous list of needs." Gerry considered for a moment. "No spouse?"

Nell shrugged. "Unlike you, I'm not one for romance. A friend who can warm my bed when called upon is all I need."

Gerry blushed.

"Sorry," Nell said. "Should I not say such things in front of you?"

Bertie walked in at that moment of all times. "My word, m'dear. Shocking poor Gerry, are you?"

Gerry laughed. "No, not at all. I did go to university, after all."

"Heavens, darling," Bertie said, settling into a seat opposite them. "Don't tell me you were the research type."

Gerry smirked at him. "I will confirm no such thing. But I can say that I have three brothers, two of whom write to me excessively and tell me far too many things that, by rights, I ought not to know. In point of fact, *they* ought not to know any of it either considering we're nextborns and considered too delicate for such things, but Seb is not quite as properly behaved as we would like. And Gavin...well, Gavin always tells me everything."

Bertie grinned. "Really, darling? Do tell. What on earth could sweet little Gavin say to shock you? I am all curiosity."

Gerry's smile was sly. "Oh, now, Bertie. You know I could never betray him like that. But if you really want to know, you might ask him sometime."

"Oh, depend upon it."

"Did you need me for anything?" Nell asked him.

"Just coming to check on you, my sweet. And to tell you I procured us a tour to another possible career option. We go tomorrow."

The tour turned out to be a factory. Nell decidedly did not like the atmosphere. The spells were all made for efficiency and the expressions on the workers were tight—either from exhaustion or unhappiness, Nell couldn't tell. At one point, she saw a woman with the exact same shade of red hair as Patience, and Nell's heart did a flip at the idea of seeing a familiar face. She quickly realized it wasn't Patience and then felt foolish for looking for a friend amongst a crowd of strangers. The thought of her friend gave her a pang as she remembered that she was unlikely to see her again.

As they left, she told Bertie that factory work was the lowest on her list.

"I certainly do not blame you there, m'dear. However, I will point out that factories are excellent places to gain some experience. If you struggle to find work immediately, you can always start out at a factory before moving on to more pleasant positions. Besides, factories are often at the forefront of magical innovation. Places like Almack's and the Royal Saloon are far grander, but tend to lean heavily on traditional spellwork. They are a little more reluctant to experiment with new designs.

"Imagine, for instance, what you observed of Miss Locke's character. She knows what works for the building and she will be disinclined to change how things are done. Factories, by their very nature, are more open to new spellwork— anything that would make their work more efficient, easy, and safe. So they are good places to start, particularly if you want to be in a position of learning new magic, or for moving upward, were you so inclined. A talented spellcaster who sets herself apart by being quick and clever could find herself being promoted to higher and better positions."

Nell pondered this lesson for days. She surprised herself by realizing she was not so opposed to the notion of working in a factory, given Bertie's explanation. After all, she had worked in unfavorable conditions in the past and had thrived. Perhaps it would not be a bad starting point. Nevertheless, Bertie had promised her one more experience, so she contented herself with keeping an open mind.

Nell was not surprised to learn that Bertie was going to Almack's too. On the night of the outing, he spent over an hour getting dressed and then came downstairs to explain to Nell her workload for the evening. He ushered her into his study and sat her down in one of the wingback chairs.

"I do apologize, m'dear, that I will be leaving you for the entire evening."

"I don't mind," she said. "Especially since you always give me something to do."

He chuckled. "Well, as it happens, I thought you might enjoy an evening off. I've neglected to give you your wages— dashed absent-minded me, I do apologize—but I can provide you with the money now if you'd like to go out on the town by yourself. If not, you are welcome to use the library or go visit one of your friends."

She was a little shocked by the offer. "You don't need to give me money," she said. "You're paying me with my lessons."

He waved his hand dismissively. "Nonsense, my sweet. I'm having far too much fun in teaching you to count it as payment."

Nell considered. Ordinarily, she would have gone to visit Patience, but she certainly couldn't do that anymore. "I might go see how Pip is doing," she said after a long moment.

Bertie gave a small smile. "Wonderful. I do hope you'll give the dear man my regards."

"Of course."

He was in the process of handing her some money when an older person Nell had never met before strode into the room. She made a guess that this was the dukex Gerry had mentioned. They were wearing a tailored suit, complete with cravat, and gentleman's shoes, but also sported a lady's turban with a feather curling around the side, pearl earrings, and a white fan. They were a short and round individual, and Nell wondered if they might be related to Bertie, for they looked as if they could be.

They glanced at Nell and turned immediately to Bertie and said, "Bertram, kindly make introductions."

Bertie stepped forward and said, "Of course, Your Grace. Allow me to present Miss Nell Birks. Nell, dear, this is my cousin, the Dukex of Molbury."

Nell curtsied, feeling nervous under the dukex's critical gaze. She wasn't sure what she was allowed to say so she stood awkwardly, waiting for instructions.

"A pleasure, Miss Birks," the dukex said with a tilt of their head. "You are young Bertram's new protege, I take it?"

"Yes, Your Grace," Bertie said.

"The same one who stepped in when Charles was met with thieves back in February?"

"Yes, er, Your Grace," Nell said when Bertie gave her an encouraging smile.

To her surprise, the dukex's steely gaze was almost kindly, for all their sternness. "I have heard many good things about you, child, from Bertram, Charles, and Geraldine. I look forward to your further acquaintance. Bertram will bring you to dinner some night soon." They said this with a nod in Bertie's direction. Then they turned to Bertie. "You look very well, child. Are you ready?"

"I just need a few more minutes with dear Nell, Your Grace. I'll only be a moment."

"The carriage is outside. Don't be long."

Nell stared after them as they walked out. She turned back to Bertie. "Are they always so intense?"

He chuckled. "Always. But don't let it worry you. They like you already." He made sure she didn't need anything else from him and then bid her good evening.

Nell waited until she heard the carriage pull away from the townhouse and then she put on her plainest coat and strode out the door. The walk to Jack's tavern made her feel strange and she worried a little that Pip might reject her in the same way Patience had. But when she finally reached the tavern, Pip wasn't there. She found Jimmy Connor, and he raised an expressive eyebrow when she asked where Pip was.

"Pip?" he said. "Jack took him out a little while ago. I don't think he'll be back for some time yet."

"Why not?"

Jimmy shrugged. "When they go out at this time of night, Pip doesn't usually come back with him. But I'm sure he'll be here tomorrow," he hastened to add.

Nell was puzzled by this. "Do you think he's gone to the old room above the butcher?"

Jimmy shook his head. "He always comes down from Jack's room every morning. But if you're wanting company," he added, leaning forward. "I'm free."

She rolled her eyes. "Thanks, but that's not the sort of company I was looking for."

He sighed. "Breaking my heart, you are."

She walked slowly back to the townhouse, confused by

Pip's absence and what Jimmy had told her. Where could Jack and Pip have possibly gone where Pip would stay behind and not return until later? She was sure it hadn't happened when she was around. Had it? Then again, she had spent most of her nights on her little mattress and had always taken for granted that Pip was with Jack. She felt uneasy, although she couldn't determine why. By the time she reached Bertie's house, she had come to the conclusion that she could trust Jack to take care of Pip and it wasn't her responsibility to worry about him anymore. But even with this resolution, she struggled to fall asleep.

The next day, as promised, Gerry came by for tea and described the evening in full detail. Nell was relieved to hear that her friend did, in fact, have quite a few admirers and had danced as much as she'd wanted.

"Didn't I tell you?" she said, nudging Gerry.

"I'm sure it has more to do with knowing Bertie and Charles and the dukex," Gerry said.

"Nonsense," Nell said.

Gerry beamed at the praise. "Are you learning any interesting theories this week?"

"Learning about Sandellini," Nell said. "And I'm doing both of these spells he invented," she added, picking up the book and handing it over.

Gerry glanced through the marked pages. "You know," she said slowly. "I have an experiment that might help explain some of it."

Nell sat up straighter. "What sort of experiment?"

"It's a spell I'm working on. I've talked to Bertie about it and I want to show it to him to see what he thinks. When I was in Tutting-on-Cress, there was this sweet spellmaster, Mr. Fenshaw, who taught me how to build spells. I used to show my work to him anytime I experimented. Bertie has offered to help, but I've had precious little time for spell experimentation since I returned to London. In any case, if you'd be open to helping me when I cast it, we can talk about how it applies to your lesson."

Nell agreed eagerly.

Gerry returned the next day and she, Nell, and Bertie gathered in Bertie's workroom. As it turned out, Gerry concentrating on her magic was a uniquely enchanting sight. She had donned an apron over her fine dress, which almost made her look common.

Gerry was exceedingly polite in her requests for assistance, and wound up doing half the work in preparing the room. When she set about putting the spell together, her face was screwed up in the most endearing expression of concentration.

The spell Gerry was working on was an expansion of a drying spell. "Gavin gave me the idea last winter," she said. "He fell into the water in the middle of November and got a frightful chill."

"*Fell*, m'dear?" Bertie said with a grin. "I did not hear it that way."

Gerry stifled her own smile. "Well, let us say he fell, poor thing. He really does get into the awfulest scrapes sometimes. He is so unaccustomed to being impetuous that any time he attempts it, he does it frightfully poorly. At any rate, he mentioned in a letter that he thought a quick drying spell that could be cast on a person would be a good invention, so I've been working on it."

Nell suspected her friend was saying most of this for her benefit. Gerry then proceeded to explain to them both—but really, Nell knew, it was being explained to her—what each component of the spell was for.

"Now," Gerry said at last. "If I might impose on you?"

"What?" Nell said.

"If I might dampen your hand a bit and then apply the spell? And don't worry," she hastened to add. "It's quite safe. At worst, the spell will not work."

"There are no dangerous materials in it, you see," Bertie added.

Nell held out her hand obligingly.

Gerry leaned closer so their shoulders were touching and then she gently flipped Nell's offered hand palm up and splashed some water onto it. Then she performed the spell and the water in Nell's palm dried up.

"Brilliant, Gerry!" Bertie said, peering over Nell's shoulder. "Quite marvelous. Will it work over a larger area?"

"It should," she replied. "And it has recasting abilities. May I?" she said to Nell.

Nell nodded. Gerry applied water from Nell's forearm down to her fingertips and recast the spell. It took a little longer, but Nell's entire arm and hand were dry within seconds.

"Genius, my darling," Bertie said. "I must say I'm impressed."

Nell was too. She couldn't believe that Gerry had invented a brand-new spell, particularly when Nell was still learning how to cast traditional ones. It was nothing like her own accidental discovery of the look-away spell; this one Gerry had designed and planned. "Is this what you would do if you were a spellmaster?"

Gerry started cleaning up and said, "I imagine the bulk of my work would be putting together common spells. But I love experimenting and designing new spells, so I would certainly incorporate that into my inventory—" She broke off and blushed. "Well, if I could, that is."

CHAPTER 9

NELL'S DAYS now fell fully into a routine. She would have breakfast with Bertie, assist him with his own spells until around lunchtime, then afterward he would teach her a lesson on a theory or teach her a new spell, and for the rest of the evening she practiced whatever spell she was still working to master. Gerry continued to visit with her during the occasional teatime.

Bertie took her to one final place to see spellcasters in action: the opera. At first, Nell had no idea why he would think this a good place for her. She did not like the stuffy sea of people around her and she did not like the jewels and silks the ladies wore. They made her feel, for once, a little out of place. Nor did she particularly like watching a performance sung in an entirely different language. It made her feel ignorant, and Nell was very uncomfortable with the notion.

But partway into the performance, Bertie leaned over and said, "See that young lady with her hair pulled back?"

He was pointing at a woman about Nell's age, dressed entirely in black, with an apron tied around her waist.

"Watch," he said.

As the song on stage built in intensity, the woman kneeled on the side of the stage, out of view from most of the audience, and cast a spell so fast that Nell couldn't keep up. An explosion sparkled on the stage in front of Nell and she jumped in surprise. Then, the spellcaster tidied her spell as quickly as she had cast it and moved back into the wings as the audience applauded the spectacle.

Nell gaped and looked at Bertie. He grinned. "Illusion spells, darling. Devilishly tricky things. A lot can go wrong. But they can be great fun. Keep an eye out for other spell-casters and see what you can observe."

She did, and saw one spellcaster perform a spell that made rain appear to fall. Another sent wind billowing across the stage, and another one levitated set pieces when they were no longer in use.

"Where do they go?" she asked, pointing to one as it was raised upward.

"I imagine they have a way to secure them. Shelves or ropes or something. More than likely there is a member of the crew up there to put it away. The spellcaster merely does the heavy lifting."

Nell was so busy watching the spellcasters that she completely ignored the opera itself and was startled when it was over.

"Well, dear?" Bertie said when they were in his carriage and heading back home.

"I loved it," she gushed. "It was incredible. I would adore working there."

He beamed. "I'm so glad, darling. Exciting place, the theater, isn't it? It has a magic all its own, quite apart from regular, everyday magic."

"Will you teach me illusion spells?" she asked.

"All in good time, my sweet. But they will certainly be a part of your repertoire eventually. Like the factories, the theaters are also at the forefront of magical innovation. I suspect that is something you would like, which is why I mention it."

Nell decided then and there that the opera would be the first place she applied for employment. The next day, she told Gerry all about it.

"Illusion spells are fascinating," Gerry agreed. "I rather think my little brother has shown a marked proficiency for them. Although he doesn't use that talent very wisely."

"Is this the one who does pranks at school?"

"That's the one." She frowned. "Goodness. I've told you all about my family. You've barely mentioned yours."

Nell shrugged. "Not much family to speak of."

"Friends?"

"Some."

"Tell me about them?"

So she told Gerry all about Pip and Jack, and even talked a bit about Patience, much as it pained her to do so.

"Do you miss them?"

Nell considered. "I do. But I suppose I always knew Pip and I might part ways eventually."

"Couldn't you invite him to tea or something?"

"I'm not sure," she said. "The last time he was here we… er…were breaking in. I'm not sure he'd be comfortable coming back."

Gerry's eyes widened. "You were?"

"You didn't know about that?"

Gerry shook her head. Nell was relieved that her friend wasn't disgusted by the information.

Nell smiled and launched into the story. By the time Gerry left, she felt as though she was even closer to her new friend. She realized with a pang that her time with Gerry was likely limited too, albeit for different reasons than her time with Pip and with Patience. She supposed that was the cost of moving up and down in society.

The next day, Gerry came with news: the dukex had invited Nell to dinner.

Nell took the invitation Gerry handed her. "Should I be nervous?"

Gerry grinned. "No, you'll do just fine. We'll all be there with you anyhow, so you won't be alone or anything."

Nell breathed out a long sigh. "Good."

"They can be frightening when you first meet them. But they're very sweet underneath it all."

"They seemed kind," Nell said.

Gerry nodded. "I think you'll like them."

Despite Gerry's advice to the contrary, Nell was nervous when she stepped into the carriage to go to dinner. She hadn't eaten outside of Bertie's townhouse since he had taken her to see the different career options. Bertie seemed to notice her anxiety because he spent much of the carriage prodding her into conversation. Although she wasn't entirely distracted from her nervousness, she was grateful to him for the effort.

When they pulled up to the dukex's townhouse, her nerves came back in full force. The townhouse was massive, as close to a palace as anything Nell had ever seen. Their little party was ushered into an opulent drawing room where four people were already seated.

Gerry turned out to be correct as Charles, Gerry, and her brother were all there as well. Mr. Hartford bowed politely to Nell and then sat quietly for most of the evening.

The dukex insisted Nell sit on the sofa beside them. "Now," they said, leaning back and looking her over with interest. "Tell me about yourself."

Nell nearly asked what they wanted to know but stopped herself. She realized the dukex was giving her the opportunity to say exactly what she wanted known. So, she placed her hands primly in her lap and said, "I was born and raised in London, Your Grace. I've wanted to learn magic for a very long time. Bertie—his lordship, rather—kindly agreed to teach me. I've been working as his assistant to repay him for the lessons. I want to work at the opera house as a spellcaster."

"No parents, I gather?"

"No, Your Grace. I never knew them. I was sort of raised by a man named Jack, but he wasn't my father. Although he was good to me and the other children he found." She wondered if she ought to be more circumspect about her humble beginnings, but reasoned privately that the dukex likely already knew of them.

The dukex's gaze flicked briefly over to Bertie and then returned to her. "Are you enjoying your lessons?"

"Yes, Your Grace," she said. "I like learning magic. And I like knowing how to read. Bertie taught me that as well."

"From what I hear, child, you have been an exemplary student. How do you like working with Bertram?"

Nell would have been irritated about being called a child, but she had heard them call Bertie the same thing, and he was older than she was. "I like it. I like seeing him perform magic. I wish I understood more of what he was doing."

They chuckled. "That is understandable. Bertram has always been very advanced when it comes to the study of magic." Their tone was unmistakably proud. "From what he has described, you have considerable talent yourself, so I imagine you will learn it all quickly."

"I hope so," she said. "I thought I'd be learning it all faster, to be honest. I didn't count on the reading lessons—not that I minded them," she added hastily. "But then memorizing the Constitutional Properties and everything. Bertie said that it is better for me to understand the theory before I learn the magic itself, and he was right. But it took forever to get to the practical lessons. I've only just started those."

Bertie spoke up. "Once you get through these initial lessons, m'dear, you will fly through the rest. I am certain."

She nodded and waited for the dukex's next question.

"Have you ever been to a dinner party?"

"No," she said. "I've mostly been at home."

"Any interest in marriage?" they said.

She was surprised by the question. "Not really," she said. "I've never had much patience or interest in romance. I do better on my own anyway."

Their mouth quirked up. "I'm of much the same mind, actually."

"Really?" she said.

They nodded. "I was married once. I have little desire in attempting it again. I much prefer to find matches for other people," they continued in a tone that was almost conspiratorial.

"Did you introduce Mr. Kentworthy and Mr. Hartford then?"

Charles laughed at the question. "No, they did not. I chanced to meet Gavin at Nesbit's Club, a fact that Julian here takes great exception to."

They sighed. "Yes, well it was rather improper. Thankfully, there was little harm done, through some strange miracle," they added, throwing an arch look in the couple's direction. "And of course, we're all focused on Geraldine's prospects. Once she is nicely settled, I shall devote my energy to Bertram."

Bertie chuckled. "You needn't worry about me, Your Grace."

"Oh, no?" they said, raising an eyebrow.

"You know I am perfectly contented."

"Don't be silly, child. You are an incurable romantic."

Bertie blushed a little but rolled his eyes good-naturedly. "Well, I am happy to wait my turn. Please do not rush for my sake."

Nell realized suddenly that she had never seen Bertie blush before. Except perhaps when Pip had dimpled at him the night they met. Had he been blushing underneath his hands when he jokingly covered up his face? She was so caught up in trying to remember that she jumped a little when the dukex tutted and said, "If you weren't a firstborn, I would have seen you married long before now."

"Yes," Bertie said. "I'm very grateful for your restraint."

Charles laughed again. "Aren't we all?" He gave the dukex a mischievous grin. "I rather think firstborns are like fine wine, Julian. We improve with age."

Mr. Hartford's mouth quirked into something that was almost a smile and he muttered good naturedly, "Ridiculous man."

Charles's grin widened.

"Best to know what you're getting into, m'dear," Bertie said to Mr. Hartford.

Mr. Hartford raised an eyebrow and said, "Yes, well, he's lucky I like fine wine."

Everyone laughed and Nell was a little surprised that the quiet young man had made a joke. She was so used to him shyly keeping to the background.

"He's very lucky," the dukex agreed. "And, no, Charles, I do not think we need to wait until Bertram becomes a proper vintage to find him a spouse."

The footman came in and announced that dinner was ready, and the teasing conversation continued as they made their way into the dining room. Nell deduced through the chatter that the dukex's concern over Gerry's prospects was stronger than their concerns about Bertie. As a nextborn, Gerry wouldn't reach her majority for another six years, and she was still dependent on her parents to take care of her. She would have to get married or find an appropriate career if she wanted security. As a firstborn, Bertie reached his majority sooner than Gerry. As he was also very wealthy, he was fully independent and didn't need to marry unless he wanted to.

Nell took this all in and was privately grateful that she didn't have to worry about such things. As an orphan, she had no idea what her birth order was, but it hardly mattered since she wasn't in her friends' social status.

She was somewhat accustomed to sumptuous dinners but was still impressed by the meal set before her on the table. Among the many dishes served were soup, lobster, asparagus and peas cooked in some sort of sauce, beetroot, goose, aspic jelly, fruit, and chocolate cream. The dukex continued to take charge of the conversation, although they seemed to make sure that everyone joined in throughout dinner. Nell relaxed a bit, no longer under the aristocrat's studious gaze.

At the end of the evening, her host bowed and said, "It was lovely to see you again, Miss Birks. I hope you will come again soon."

"Thank you for having me," she said. She hesitated and then added, "I was worried you might look down on me. I find it odd that you and Bertie are so nice to me even though you are so much higher socially than I am."

They smiled. "I prefer judging a person by their character rather than their birth. It is, after all, merely a coincidence that you were picked up by this Jack person rather than brought to an orphanage to be adopted by a couple like Charles and Gavin. Moreover, a person who knows how to steal from a man but chooses to rescue him instead is most decidedly not beneath my notice. That is why I choose to admire your character, and I suspect Bertram is of the same mind."

She glanced back at Bertie. He smiled at her. "It's true, m'dear. That and our first meeting—well, you both quite impressed me then too."

"Both?" the dukex said.

"My friend Pip," Nell explained. "Bertie offered to teach him magic too, but he preferred to stay with Jack. It's a shame, really. I'm sure you would have liked him too."

"I'm sure I would," they said. They gave Bertie an unreadable look. "I hope I have occasion to meet him sometime."

Nell doubted that, but didn't think it would be polite to

say. She thanked the dukex again and walked out the door. Bertie followed a few moments later, having talked to his cousin briefly first.

"Well," Bertie said, as the carriage rattled down the road. "What did you think of your first dinner party?"

"It was exhausting," Nell said with a laugh. "But the food was good. I like your cousin."

"I'm very glad, darling," he said. "I was sure they would like you too."

CHAPTER 10

A FEW DAYS after the dukex's dinner party, Charles sent over a little card inviting Nell to tea. While Nell was surprised by this, Bertie seemed to have expected it.

"Ah good," he said when she showed him the card. "He managed it then."

Completely mystified, Nell followed Bertie's lead in putting on the outerwear requisite to leaving the house and they walked down the street to Charles's address.

Charles greeted her saying, "I'm so glad you could make it, darling," as if Nell had a full social calendar. Then he ushered her into his sitting room.

Seated in the sitting room was a young woman a little older than Nell who had dark brown skin, large dark eyes, and thick hair pulled into a simple updo. Her clothing was plain and without frills but, Nell noted, it was also clean and in good condition.

Nell executed a little curtsy as Charles introduced them.

"Nell, dear, this is Miss Betsy Holgraf. Miss Holgraf, this is Miss Birks."

Miss Holgraf cocked an eyebrow at Nell's curtsy. "Charmed, I'm sure," she said in a tone that Nell suspected was sarcasm.

Charles chuckled and gestured for Nell to sit. "Miss Holgraf works at the theater, darling. She has agreed to come and talk to you about the possibility of working there."

Nell sat up straighter. "Really?"

"Mr. Kentworthy has informed me that you are a talented spellcaster."

"I'm still learning," Nell said. "But I'm a quick learner and I already have some of the basic spells mastered."

Miss Holgraf's eyebrows rose a little at this sentence. She turned to Charles. "Might I speak to her alone, please?"

Charles glanced at Nell. When she nodded, he bowed and he and Bertie left the room.

"I hope I can speak plainly, Miss Birks," Miss Holgraf said.

"Of course," Nell said, feeling anxious by the woman's abruptness.

"I had some misgivings about Mr. Kentworthy's request. You see, I have no interest in training a highborn lady in hard work and a less than glamorous lifestyle." She tilted her head a bit. "But I'm beginning to think that isn't what you are."

Nell was surprised. "No," she said. "I'm not a highborn lady at all."

"What we do at the theater is exciting," Miss Holgraf went on. "We dazzle audiences, we work behind velvet curtains. But you will be on your feet for hours at a time. You will be expected to work quickly and without mistakes. You will live at the theater. You will be sharing a room with another spellcaster. There will be no servants to wait on you. You would get one day off every other week. Even when there is no show going on, you will share some of the responsibility in keeping the theater in good condition and rehearsing spells." She paused. "I'm not interested in wasting my time with someone who is accustomed to being waited on and being dressed and going to balls. This is not a step up in society."

Nell practically laughed at the woman's misconception of her. "I can assure you I don't expect to be waited on."

"You're living with a viscount," the woman returned. "Mr. Kentworthy said you're working as the gentleman's spell-casting assistant. How long have you been working for him?"

"A few months?"

"Is he unkind to you?"

"No, not at all."

"I'm struggling to understand why you would choose the theater instead. The theater pays a decent wage, but I doubt it pays as well as the position you have now. I have no desire to train someone only to have her leave when the work is too tiring."

"I most certainly won't do that."

Miss Holgraf pursed her lips. "Quite frankly, I'm less than convinced. Come back to me when you've worked for this viscount for a longer time, if you're still interested. A few months in one position does not inspire much confidence. Most people who work at the theater work there for the rest of their lives. Besides, I have no open positions at the present time."

She stood and Nell grappled for a way to change her mind, but she couldn't think of anything. She couldn't even offer to cast a spell for the woman's benefit; she was still learning the basics and she doubted that would be impressive. Besides, Miss Holgraf was right: Nell's position with Bertie looked perfect. But Bertie had never spoken of making her a permanent placement in his household—if anything, he had done the exact opposite, taking her to different potential places of employment. Bertie clearly saw her time with him as temporary. She felt panic build inside her as Miss Holgraf bid her goodbye and strode out of the room.

Bertie hurried in. "How did it go, darling?"

Nell felt like she might cry. "I…" Her voice cracked and she looked away, embarrassed.

His face instantly turned to sympathy. "Oh, m'dear. I am sorry. She didn't take you on? Not even an audition?"

Nell shook her head. "She didn't understand why I would choose the theater when I have a perfectly good position here. I know this position is temporary, but it's a little difficult to explain that. She said to try again when I've been here for longer than a few months."

"What a wrench," Bertie said. He sat down beside her. "Well, it was a bit of a gamble to expect the first attempt would be a success." He patted her hand. "As for this position being temporary, I hope you know that I have no intention of sending you away. You've been a wonderful assistant."

She sniffed, feeling a little buoyed by the compliment. "Really?"

"Invaluable, my sweet. I don't know how I got by without an assistant all these years." He gave her an encouraging smile. "How about this: you stay on for as long as you'd like and when you get tired of this work, you can try again—either at the theater or elsewhere—and I shall gladly keep you employed until you find something else."

This offer made Nell feel weepy all over again.

"Why don't you take the rest of the day off, m'dear?"

She accepted his offer and when she was finally in the privacy of her own room, she allowed herself to cry. She felt foolish for putting all of her hopes on one position, for expecting to get the job simply because she wanted it. She consoled herself that Bertie was inviting her to stay on as his assistant. And Miss Holgraf *had* said she could try again when she'd been working for Bertie longer. She dried her tears, resolving to do just that.

For the next couple of weeks, Nell threw herself into her work. She wasn't accustomed to failing, especially failing before she'd even begun. So she set out to prove Miss Holgraf wrong. She stayed up late into the night, studying the books Bertie assigned to her, and she practiced every spell she was taught with grim determination.

Just when the pain of rejection was beginning to lose some of its edge, Nell received another blow. This one from an unlikely source: Gerry.

Nell had been helping Bertie set up for a spell when Gerry came bustling into the study. "Oh!" she said breathlessly. "I have such news!"

"Good heavens, m'dear," Bertie said. "Whatever is the matter?"

"It's the most wonderful—well, I'd better not get ahead of myself. I need your advice."

"Sit, darling. Have some tea. Tell us everything."

Gerry pulled a letter out of her reticule. "I just received this letter. It's from Mr. Fenshaw in Tutting-on-Cress. Do you remember the sweet little spellmaster I told you about?"

"The one who taught you how to build your own spells?" Nell said.

"That's the one. Well, he wants to retire. He's going to sell his shop. He listed the price here and, well, he says that he would very much like me to manage it."

Nell was stunned. "Can you do that?"

"Well, that's what I'm here to find out. What do you think I should do, Bertie?" Gerry asked.

"Do? Well, darling, I think you should certainly move to Tutting-on-Cress. The offer to manage a spell shop is not going to come around again, I daresay."

"Oh, good," she said, letting out a relieved breath. "That's what I'd hoped you'd say."

"The question is, how to go about telling your family that you're going into trade?"

Gerry threw back her head and laughed. "Oh, won't John be scandalized!" she said. When she regained her composure, she said, "Mama will not exactly be thrilled, I think. And it will be an awful wrench to go with less money, of course. But, oh, running a spell shop all on my own! Can you imagine it?" She grabbed Nell's hands and whirled her around the room, much like she had when she was invited to Almack's. Then she stopped and turned back to Bertie. "I'll have to tell Gavin. Oh goodness. And Charles. Oh. And the dukex. What on earth will they say about it?"

"I'll have them to dinner," Bertie said. "All of you. Then you can make the announcement."

Gerry clapped her hands in excitement and then left the room as suddenly as she had arrived.

Nell turned to Bertie. "Where is Tutting-on-Cress?"

Bertie was staring in Gerry's wake, looking thoughtful. "Hm? Oh, I believe it's in Bedfordshire, m'dear. About fifty miles from London."

Nell felt her heart sink. "Oh."

Bertie gave her an understanding smile. "I'll miss her too. Thankfully, I've been told that Gerry is an exceptional correspondent, so we will still hear from her."

Nell tried returning her attention to the spell. "Do you think her family will approve? She told me once that it will be a step down in society and her parents were unlikely to accept that."

"It is difficult to say. I've never met her parents, m'self."

"If they're anything like her brother, I have a hard time believing they'll approve of anything. He's so very serious."

Bertie barked out a laugh. "Actually, I expect Gavin will be the most supportive member of her family."

"Really?"

"He *is* serious and a bit fretful, poor thing. So I imagine he will have concerns about the venture. But despite his gravity, he's a very kind soul. He will want her to be happy."

Nell was surprised to learn that Bertie was correct. At the dinner Bertie hosted, Mr. Hartford had a list of concerns—it was the most Nell had heard him talk in their months of acquaintanceship—but he seemed pained in having to point them out. He didn't seem at all concerned about the step down in society, but rather worried about his sister's financial stability and how she might support herself. He also pointed out that no one in their family could afford to help her purchase the shop. Nell had forgotten that detail of the offer. She remembered what Gerry had once told her about their family not actually being so very high-born.

In the end, the only person who was truly worried about Gerry's social prospects was the Dukex of Molbury. But after they gave a small speech insisting Gerry be prepared for this decision to be a permanent one, they gave their approval.

Charles wound up having solutions for the majority of his fiancé's concerns, announcing that he had been looking into property in the area already and was prepared to purchase a house for himself and Mr. Hartford, and inviting Gerry to live with them. Then Bertie surprised everyone by offering to buy the spell shop and hiring Gerry to manage it.

The evening ended with the decision that Gerry, her brother, Charles, and the dukex would all leave for Tutting-on-Cress within the fortnight. The first three would settle there, while the dukex would only stay until Charles and Mr. Hartford were married. Nell was relieved that Bertie declined to go too, even though Charles suggested he join the party in their move to the country.

"I am certain I can manage the business from here," he said.

Everyone seemed delighted by the plans—except Nell. She went to bed feeling frustrated and jealous, and guilty for feeling that way. She hated the idea of Gerry leaving to go to the country; it seemed unlikely that she would ever see her friend again. But she also knew it was exactly what Gerry wanted. She tossed and turned all night, agitated at the thought that her friendships seemed doomed to end in separation, one way or another.

As the party's imminent departure approached, Bertie seemed to get in a progressively more uncharacteristically poor mood—which is to say, he was restless and indecisive, while still maintaining his usual cheerful demeanor.

"Are you all right?" Nell asked.

He waved his hand airily. "Oh, yes, my sweet. Perfectly fine."

She raised an eyebrow dubiously.

He chuckled. "Well, I should confess that I'm a little flustered at the thought of living so far away from Charlie. We've always lived quite close, you see. I don't like the idea of this distance, although I suppose it was inevitable. We always knew we'd find spouses, but I'd rather hoped that we'd settle near each other."

"I know what you mean," she said. "I always thought Pip and I would be close forever. My friend Patience says that's part of growing up."

"I daresay she's right. But between you and me, darling, I'm not overly fond of this aspect of growing up. I always thought Charlie and I would grow old together, in our own way." He sighed. "Ah well."

Nell considered this for a long moment. "Why don't you move to the country with them?"

"I have several reasons for that. One of which is that I am sometimes called upon to help the crown and Parliament with my expertise. Another is that I have a tendency to become very antisocial when I get involved in projects. Being in London means that it is difficult for me to be too antisocial as I am forever being invited to gatherings. I worry about moving to the country and becoming an eccentric recluse." He chuckled at the thought. "But I should also admit that I didn't think it would be fair to you."

"What?" she said, startled. "You're staying in London because of me?"

"Only partly, my sweet. As unsure as I am about how I would do in the country, I am certain you would not enjoy country life very much."

"You're not wrong," she admitted. "What about when I find a position elsewhere?"

"Then I shall reconsider my options," he said simply.

Bertie seemed to think that put an end to the matter, but Nell was not satisfied with the conclusion. When the fortnight was up, they bid their friends goodbye with a farewell dinner, Gerry promised Nell she would write, and then Gerry, Charles, Mr. Hartford, and the dukex left London. Nell expected Bertie's social calendar to empty now that Charles and the dukex were gone, but he wound up being even busier than before. He kept long hours, flitting in and out of the house for social commitments, and spending practically every moment he was at home on some magical project or other. He did not require Nell to mimic his long hours, but she found herself uneasy with the prospect of leaving him alone. Together, they'd work on spells until the early hours of the morning more nights than not.

CHAPTER 11

AFTER NEARLY A MONTH of Bertie burying himself in social commitments and magical projects, Nell finally decided it was time to do something. She knew better than most what it was like to lose someone who felt like family. She needed to find another position so Bertie could be free to move to the country.

She tried to see herself at the restaurant, the ballroom, or even the factory, but she kept coming back to the idea of the theater. She thought back to her conversation with Miss Holgraf. The woman worried that Nell would be hired and then leave shortly after. Perhaps if she explained that her circumstances had changed, and that she still wanted to work there, then maybe Miss Holgraf would believe her to be in earnest. She remembered Bertie's surprise that Nell hadn't even been given an audition. Perhaps she could request one?

She waited until Bertie left for a garden party that he apologetically explained would take most of the day, and then she went to the theater. She found her way to a stage door located toward the back of the building and, after a long moment of hesitation, let herself inside.

An old man sat on the other side of the door. He looked up at her with curiosity.

"Might I see Miss Holgraf?" she said.

He snorted. "Miss Holgraf indeed. Stay here. I'll go get her." He wandered away and she stood in the dark hallway, trying not to look too excited by her own daring.

When he returned, Miss Holgraf was following him, looking confused. Her confusion cleared when she saw Nell. "Miss Birks," she said.

"May I talk to you for a minute?"

"Very well. Come with me." She led the way into a small room filled with equipment. Nell recognized some of it as the same magical equipment that Bertie used, but the rest was unfamiliar to her. Miss Holgraf closed the door behind them and leaned against a table, looking at Nell expectantly.

Nell took a deep breath. "I know that it's only been a couple of months since we last talked and that's probably not nearly as much time as you expected, but I've been thinking about it, and I realized there were some things about my situation that I didn't have a chance to explain."

"Very well," she said again, sounding a little less cold this time.

Nell was relieved by the slight thaw in the woman's tone. She continued, "I was born on the streets. I'll admit that I'm not proud of my history, but I did what I needed to survive. A few years ago, I decided I wanted to make an honest living and I started doing odd-jobs around town. Bertie—that is, Lord Finlington—was kind enough to take me on as a student. I've been working as his assistant while he teaches me, which you already knew. But the arrangement was always meant to be temporary. I'm sure that seems hard to believe since, as you pointed out, I'm currently living in very fine conditions. But…it isn't where I belong. I've been trying to find my place in the world for years. I know it's with magic work—I feel that it must be. But not with Bertie. For one thing, that life really is too fine for me. I'm not accustomed to leisure. And besides…besides, Bertie is likely moving out of

London soon. I'm not sure when, but it's bound to happen sooner or later. I don't have any mind to leave London, nor do I have any interest in making him stay here on my account."

She took another deep breath to steady her nerves, pleased that the woman hadn't interrupted. "I'm asking you to give me another chance. An audition, perhaps? I'm not as well educated in magic as I'd like to be, but if I can at least know what you're looking for then I can have something to work towards."

Miss Holgraf stared at her for a long moment. Finally, she said, "I must admit that when you didn't come to the theater yourself to demand an opportunity, I felt sure I had been right about you. I'm more concerned about the likelihood of you staying on than your education." She pursed her lips. "I actually prefer it if my spellcasters don't know very much when they come into the job. I want natural talent, of course. That's a must. And I want a good work ethic. But people who come in knowing all sorts of spells usually have to unlearn everything before I'm satisfied. That is harder to train than someone who has a good grounding in the basics."

Nell hardly dared to breathe. "Really?"

The other woman looked amused. "Yes, really. Let's see what you can do. If you're up to scratch, I might be convinced to reconsider." Her mouth twisted a bit. "And as it happens, your timing is rather good. One of my spellcasters got his sweetheart pregnant, so her parents are making him work on their farm instead of with me. He was pretty sloppy anyway, so I'm not exactly bothered by it. If you're any good, then I might be better off for his leaving. What spells have you mastered?"

It took Nell a moment to register the sudden change in topic. "Levitation, lateral movement, quick heat spell, quick dry spell, er…"

Miss Holgraf waved a hand. "That'll do. Give me a

moment." She began busying herself with pulling out pieces of equipment and laying them on an empty table. Then she said, "I've laid out everything you need. Perform a levitation spell for me."

Nell did and then, at the other woman's direction, also cast a quick heat spell.

Miss Holgraf picked up a well-worn book and leafed through the pages. Then she handed the book to Nell. "What can you tell me about this one?"

Nell studied the spell on the page. She was incredibly grateful that Bertie had insisted on a theory-based learning. "I can see that it involves levitation. That sigil there would help to counterbalance a heavy object. It looks like there are measurements involved, I'm guessing to direct the magic where to place the object?" She glanced up.

"Very good. Anything else?"

Nell frowned. "Well, there's a sigil here that I don't recognize. But the placement suggests it's an important element."

"Correct. That designates it as an illusion spell."

"Oh!" Nell said. "I've never done an illusion spell."

"Let's see how fast you can learn one then." Miss Holgraf went on to explain that the spell was designed to give the illusion of an object levitating, without actually moving said object. "We use this one for performers. We won't be practicing on a performer, of course. You can use this to practice on." She pointed to a coat rack to the side of the room.

When she didn't go on, Nell assumed she was supposed to do as much of the spell as she could figure out on her own. She pulled the coat rack to the center of the room and prepared the spell around it. When she chalked out the sigil, she glanced up at Miss Holgraf. "Is there anything particular I need to do?"

"You're doing rather well, actually," the woman replied. "But yes, there is. For illusion spells, you need to do two hand gestures at the same time." She showed Nell a complicated motion with one hand while the other hand indicated the direction the rack was supposed to go in.

Nell mimicked the movement. "Like that?"

"Close." Miss Holgraf repeated it.

After Nell had copied it correctly, she cast the spell. The coat rack stayed in its circle, but a transparent form floated upward.

"Not bad," Miss Holgraf said as she walked around the transparent form. "Could be stronger, but you did get it on the first try. You're teachable. That's the important thing." She looked back at the spell on the floor. "Why don't you go ahead and clean it up and set the room to rights for me? I want to go talk to the stage manager."

Nell got to work in cleaning up. Remembering the spell-caster she had seen in the wings, she did what she could do to be both thorough and speedy. She was pleased that she had thought of speed because Miss Holgraf was only gone for a couple of minutes. She walked in, followed by a tall, thin man, right when Nell was putting the last few things away.

"Excellent," Miss Holgraf said. "Well, Mr. Courtney. I think I've found our replacement."

Mr. Courtney said, "That was fast, even for you, Betsy."

Miss Holgraf shrugged. "I've been turning people down for months. This one showed up at the right time."

"Can you start in a week?" he said to Nell.

"Yes, sir," Nell said.

"Very good. Betsy can discuss the terms with you and when you should return." With that, he left.

Nell stared after him. "Is that it? I have the job?"

Miss Holgraf gave her a small smile. "You had the job when you set up the illusion spell properly. I would have hired you even if it hadn't gone well. You take direction well and you learn quickly. The fact that you cleaned up your work so fast makes me feel even more confident with the decision."

Nell could hardly believe her ears. "Thank you, Miss Holgraf."

"Call me Betsy. Everyone does. What was your name again?"

"Nell."

"Nell," Betsy repeated. "I can remember that. You're sure you're all right to come down from such nice living quarters?"

Nell smiled. "I've been spoiled the past few months. But I'm used to being on my own. I'm not worried."

"Good." She paused. "I think I was mistaken in you, Nell. I'm very pleased to be wrong." Then she gave her a grin. "Come back this time next week and we'll get you settled in."

Nell thanked her and made her way outside. She practically ran back to Bertie's house. Then she spent an hour pacing, wishing Bertie was home so she could tell him her news. It wound up being a very long day as Bertie didn't return home until after sunset. She practically pounced on him when he walked in the door.

"Good heavens, m'dear," he said when she'd told him the news. "This is the most wonderful news I've heard in a month. Let's celebrate."

He canceled his plans for the evening and they enjoyed a leisurely dinner together as Nell told him how the audition had gone.

"I'm so dashed proud of you," he said, beaming at her. "You really are a remarkable person, darling."

Nell beamed at the praise.

"How long have you been planning this?"

She shifted in her seat. "Not long. But it's been coming on gradually for a while."

He raised his eyebrows questioningly.

She sighed. "You're unhappy. I can tell. I don't want you staying in London for my sake when you clearly want to be somewhere else."

He gave her a rueful smile. "Oh dear," he said. "I suppose I wasn't as subtle as I thought."

"I'm not sure anyone else will have noticed. But you've been busying yourself with...well, everything." She paused. "It's easier to forget you miss someone when you're too busy to think."

He chuckled. "That was the hope at any rate."

She hesitated a minute before saying, "Are you in love with Charles?"

He gave her a broad grin. "You sweet thing. No, I'm not. I love him very dearly, but I'm not pining for him."

She leaned her cheek on her palm and, feeling bold, said, "Do you plan to get married, Bertie? You didn't seem to want your cousin to find you a spouse."

He took a sip of his wine. "I've always considered myself the marrying kind," he said. "But I confess...I'm not sure if it will ever happen."

"Why not?"

"Well...to be perfectly frank, darling, I got a bit careless with my heart and lost it. Frightfully inconvenient, really, but there it is."

Nell frowned in confusion. "What?"

He chuckled again. "Don't mind me, my sweet. It isn't important anyway. Now, let's talk about this next week, shall we? I'm happy to spend this time teaching you whatever you might wish to learn, but you also deserve a rest, if you'd like it. You've worked so frightfully hard. And I don't expect you'll have much rest once you go to work in the theater."

She was surprised by the change of subject but she decided not to press him. "Thank you. If you have any lessons that might help me, I would appreciate it. But otherwise, I'd be happy to just assist you until I leave." She paused a moment and then said, "And, of course, I can continue paying off what I owe you after I go to work."

He gave a little frown. "What are you talking about,

m'dear? The arrangement was that you would work as my assistant in exchange for lessons. You've done everything I've asked of you. I have no complaints about your work."

"Well, the dresses and the lodging—"

"Darling, the dresses were gifts. And lodging is considered a part of one's pay if one works in the household staff, as you do."

"Oh," she said.

"It would hardly be kind of me to buy you expensive things without giving you so much as a choice in the matter, and then asking you to pay me for them later."

She shrugged. "I thought that's how it was done. Jack never told us how much things cost until afterwards. It always took me quite a while to pay him back for what I owed him. Some people never finish paying him back."

His expression sharpened. "Is that so, m'dear? Well, well. I cannot entirely say I'm surprised. He does seem a crafty fellow, doesn't he?"

She laughed. "He was always fair about it, so I can't say I minded. Thank you, Bertie."

"Of course, dearest," he said.

The next morning, Bertie told her that he had more social events to attend and that he would be gone most of the day.

"Perhaps you should consider moving to…wherever Gerry and Charles live now," she said.

He smiled. "I can assure you that I'm considering it, m'dear. And I will take care to not overdo my social calendar so much in the future. But as you can imagine, I don't have any practical experiments to do today, though I expect I could use your help tomorrow."

"Would you mind if I went to go visit Pip?"

He looked at her in surprise. "Of course not, m'dear. You needn't ask for permission. Please give the dear man my regards."

She thanked him, put on a coat, and left. She hoped Pip

would be there this time. As it was earlier in the day, she felt it was reasonable to assume he would be. Usually, at this time of day, Jack was sending everyone out on their assignments. Still, she had been confident he'd be there the last time she visited too. When she arrived, she approached the barman and asked if he knew where Pip was.

"Don't think he's come downstairs yet," he replied, nodding to the stairs that led to Jack's room. He didn't seem surprised to see her and Nell wondered if he'd even noted her absence.

She took a seat at a table facing the stairs and waited. Eventually, she saw Jack coming down the stairs. He, unlike the barman, was surprised to see her.

"Well," he said. "I didn't expect to see you here again."

"I came to visit Pip," she said.

He smiled. "Of course. He'll be coming down shortly. Late to get out of bed, that one," he added with a wink. He walked off to talk to some of his people and assign tasks for the day.

A little while later, Pip walked slowly down the stairs. She quickly crossed the room to greet him.

He gaped at her. "What are you doing here?" he said. "Is everything all right?"

"Of course, silly," she said. "I just wanted to come visit you."

He relaxed. "Oh. That was nice of you." He glanced behind her. "I'd better go see what Jack wants me to do today. I'll be back." She watched him walk to Jack and receive instructions. Jack pulled Pip forward into a kiss before letting him go. "Come on," he said when he returned to her. "I'm on Hyde Park today. You can walk me there."

He set a brisk pace as they walked down the street together. Nell watched him, getting a good look at her friend. He had always been slender, but she thought he looked a little gaunt now. There were circles under his eyes and his lips were noticeably chapped. She remembered Pip had a bad habit of chewing on them.

"Are you all right?" she asked.

He shot her a startled look. "'Course," he said. "Why wouldn't I be?"

"I don't know," she said. "You look different."

He shrugged. "Nothing's changed about me," he said. "But tell me about yourself. How is living with the viscount?"

"It's been wonderful. He's so nice."

He nodded.

"I'm only staying with him for another week, though."

"Why?"

"I just got a job as a spellcaster at the opera," she said, unable to keep herself from skipping a step.

Pip, to her surprise, stopped in his tracks. "At the opera?" he said. "Why there?"

"Bertie took me to show me possible careers for spellcasters and I sort of…fell in love with it."

"You start in a week?" he said, looking troubled.

"Yes," she said. She grabbed his hand. "You should come visit me. I'll be living there. They have dormitories for their staff."

He visibly relaxed. "That's good," he said. "I'll see about visiting. It…sort of depends on what Jack says, you know."

"I'm sure he wouldn't mind."

He chewed his lip and continued walking.

Nell fell into step beside him. She wanted to ask him why he hadn't been there when she'd visited before, but she couldn't think of a way to phrase it that wouldn't sound accusatory. After all, he wasn't obligated to be around just in case she came to visit. In the end, she reminded herself it wasn't her business and it was no longer her job to keep track of him, and they continued the rest of the walk in silence.

CHAPTER 12

AFTER A WEEK HAD PASSED, Nell took a little trunk that Bertie had purchased for her, packed up her few belongings, bid Bertie a grateful and fond goodbye, and then strode off to her next adventure.

Betsy met her inside the stage door and walked her up many flights of stairs to the dormitories. "You'll be sharing a room with me," she explained. "But don't worry too much. I'm usually not here."

"Why not?" Nell couldn't help but ask.

Betsy smirked. "I usually spend the night with my sweetheart. You'll be meeting them later today."

Betsy then proceeded to take her on a full tour of the building. Nell got to see the dressing rooms, the lobby, the wings, the orchestra pit, and even got to walk high up in the theater in what Betsy called the fly loft. Along the way, Betsy introduced Nell to the other spellcasters, crew members, dancers, and singers. Betsy's sweetheart turned out to be a person around Bertie's age who wore their hair in long honey-colored plaits. They had pale skin, large blue eyes, and a friendly demeanor. Betsy introduced them as Mx. Harriet.

"Call me Harriet," they said. "Betsy just says that so you don't assume I'm a woman."

Nell smiled and shook Harriet's hand, hoping she'd found another friend.

Before the first performance, Betsy checked all of the magical supplies, making sure they had enough stock and that everything was in good shape. She explained that Nell wouldn't be responsible for all of the supplies, only the ones for the spells she was assigned to cast. Apparently, Betsy was the Lead Spellcaster for the theater, in charge of training and managing all of the in-house spellcasters, so she had more responsibilities than most.

Nell learned that there were spellcasters backstage to handle the spells during the performance, as well as spellcasters at the front of the house to cast cooling spells when there were large crowds and to maintain the lighting spells throughout the building. The backstage spellcasters, which Nell was relieved to learn she would be, were assigned tracks: there were two responsible for scenery and prop movement, one assigned to each of the leading performers, three assigned to the chorus, one assigned to the orchestra, two in charge of special effects, and one who floated, filling in as needed. As Betsy was the Lead Spellcaster, she typically took on the floating position. But throughout the first week, she said she would show Nell a different track each night, sending the usual spellcaster to the float position.

During her first night in the theater, Nell trailed behind Betsy as she wound her way backstage. Betsy turned at the front of one well-lit room.

"This is where the smaller parts do their makeup and costumes and everything," she explained. "Some of us are assigned to work with the performers, you see. We'll cast spells for them during the performance to make their voices louder, things like that. If you're in charge of the smaller parts, you'll want to check on any spells you've set up back-stage and then come around to this room to check in with your performer. Go over what spells you're going to use. That kind of thing. I'll show you what I mean."

Betsy showed her around the room and then moved back out to the hallway. Nell was about to follow her out of the room when someone rounded the corner and bumped into her. He caught her shoulders as she stumbled backward. "Sorry about that," he said. He cocked his head and looked her up and down. "Don't recall seeing you before. New?"

Betsy showed up at the stranger's elbow. "I told Archie he never should have rouged your cheeks. We won't be able to get rid of you now."

He gave her a wide grin. "Admit it. You're delighted."

She laughed. "Nell, this is Lino Bowles. Lino, this is Nell Birks. As you guessed, she's new. Spellcaster."

He dropped his hands from her shoulders and gave a little bow. "Pleasure."

"Do you work in the theater too?"

He leaned against the wall. "Nah, I work—how did Harriet put it?—adjacent to the theater."

Nell frowned at him, confused.

"He works in the courtyard," Betsy said. "With the harlots and street vendors."

"Oh," Nell said.

She gave Lino a quick once-over. He was a tall, slender person. He might have been described as gangly except he had a sort of gracefulness to him that rejected that description. He had light brown skin and a mop of dark curly hair. His dark eyes were framed with long lashes and he had freckles speckled across his nose and cheeks. He was wearing his shirt unbuttoned, providing a view of his chest.

Nell gave him a smirk. "And what sort of wares do you sell then?"

He laughed. "The best of wares, Nelly. I'm a very desirable product."

A large man loomed in the doorway behind Nell. "Ah," he said in a husky voice. "You again, is it?"

Lino tilted his head in a coquettish angle. "You know I can't resist you, Archie."

The other man scoffed. "I rather think it's the other way around, you rascal. Come on, then. Same as before?"

Lino slipped around Nell and through the door, wrapping his arm around Archie's bicep. "And perhaps a little something extra?"

"Like you need it," Archie mumbled, but led the way into the room.

Nell looked at Betsy. "What was that about? Do the harlots usually come inside?"

Betsy smiled. "Most of them would be afraid of being sent right back out again. I don't know how he does it. Probably charms his way in. Archie found him outside in the courtyard one night and offered him five shillings to experiment with a new makeup look. Lino took it and then came right back the next day, saying whatever Archie did had gotten Lino the handsomest tip he'd seen in months. Or something like that. So now he comes in more nights than not and Archie does...whatever he wants, I guess."

"No one minds?" Nell said, following Betsy down the hall.

Betsy shrugged. "They're both happy and Lino knows to keep out of trouble."

Later, she spotted Lino as he sauntered back out of the room. His eyes were now lined with kohl and there was a slight rouge to his cheeks. He saw her looking and winked.

For the first week, as promised, Betsy showed Nell different tracks. Then she sat Nell down and taught her the spells required for one of the scenery spellcasters.

"They're the simplest," she explained.

So, starting the second week, Nell did half of the spells

required for set movement, with Betsy at her side to make sure nothing went wrong.

Halfway through the week, Betsy clapped her on the shoulder and said, "You're a natural. I'll go back to floating, but wave me down if you need anything."

It was frightening to be on her own so early, but she adored the trust Betsy had already given her. By the end of the second week, Betsy assured her she was ready to learn the next track.

The only downside to theater life was that she felt very much like an outsider. She liked Betsy and Harriet, but didn't feel confident in claiming their friendship. Everyone at the theater felt like one large family and Nell wasn't sure she fit. She got the sense they were all waiting to see if they liked her before accepting her as one of their own. Once again, she found herself missing people she'd left behind. Now she not only had Patience and Pip to miss, she had Gerry and Bertie, too.

When she received her first full day off, she waited until she was sure Bertie would be up, and went to call on him. She was disappointed to find him out of the house. The footman, Thomas, offered to show her into Bertie's study, but she had no interest in cooling her heels, waiting for Bertie to return.

She stood on the stoop, debating what to do. It was too late in the day to try to find Pip at the tavern. She briefly considered going to see Patience, but immediately rejected the notion, afraid of being turned away again. Finally, she opted to stroll through London alone. By the time she made it back to the theater, she was feeling very lonely and sorry for herself. She felt even worse when she remembered that Bertie would likely be moving soon.

One afternoon on her third week at the theater, she was delighted when Pip came to visit. He looked just as subdued as he had when she'd gone to see him, but she was pleased that he had actually come all the way out to talk to her. She immediately introduced him to Betsy and Harriet.

"You're very pretty," Harriet commented. "And you look a little familiar. Have I seen you somewhere before?"

"What?" Pip said, looking alarmed.

"They say that to everyone they find attractive," Betsy said. "Don't pay them any attention."

Harriet offered to let Pip sit in a corner backstage to see the performance. "Mind," they said. "I'll need to clear it with Mr. Courtney, but he usually agrees. I have him wrapped around my little finger."

"Thank you," Nell said before Pip could respond. "That would be wonderful, wouldn't it, Pip?"

"Thank you," Pip said quietly.

Harriet led Pip to the promised corner of the wings. Content that he was safe and out of the way, Nell went through her routine of checking through her spell equipment. Some time later, she went to go see how Pip was doing and was surprised to see Lino standing with him. The taller man was leaning down to talk quietly to her friend. Pip looked frightened and was chewing his lip. Nell was surprised; Lino didn't strike her as the intimidating type. She walked over to see what was wrong.

"You can't go on like this, love," Lino was saying softly. "It's practically killing you."

"There's nothing you can do," Pip said in an agitated tone. "It's kind of you to offer, but you know I couldn't possibly— Nell!" He broke off at the sight of her, looking as if he might be sick.

Lino abruptly straightened and turned. He gave her a broad grin. "Oh, it's you, Nelly. This a friend of yours?"

"This is Pip," Nell said. "I didn't know you two knew each other."

Lino seemed to hesitate for a moment. "Not exactly acquaintances. More along the lines of knowing *of* each other." He paused. "After all, everyone knows who Jack Reid is. Impossible to know who Jack is without knowing about Pip here."

Nell wasn't sure she believed him, though she didn't want to say so.

Pip was looking distinctly uncomfortable. He lurched away from Lino and said, "I'd better go. Thank your friend for me, but I really can't stay through the whole performance. Jack will be wondering where I am." He glanced furtively at Lino. "It was good to see you, Nelly. I'm glad you've found where you belong at last."

Nell forced herself to smile and gave him a hug. "Do you want me to walk you out?"

"I can lead him out," Lino said. "I'm on my way anyway."

Nell was about to step in and insist on going herself when Pip surprised her by saying, "Thank you. No need to take Nell away from her work." He murmured a quick goodbye and walked away.

Lino strolled after Pip.

Nell was completely mystified. And Pip didn't return for another visit.

CHAPTER 13

ABOUT A WEEK after Pip's visit, Nell received an invitation to tea from Bertie when she was available. She was so excited to see him again that she asked Betsy if she could take the next day off.

"I'll be sure to come back in time for the performance," she said.

Betsy agreed, provided Nell work extra hours later in the week to make up the time.

The next morning, she hurried to Bertie's house. When she arrived, she was surprised to find Charles there.

"Nell!" he said, greeting her. "How delightful to see you. How is theater life?"

"Good heavens, Charlie," Bertie said. "Let the dear girl breathe. Come in, my sweet. Tell us everything."

She sat down and described her life at the theater. "What are you doing in town?" she asked Charles when she was done.

Bertie laid a hand on Charles's arm before he could speak. "I've decided to move to Tutting-on-Cress as well," he said. "Charlie has been helping me arrange everything."

Nell was torn between relief and sadness at the news. She had expected it, but to have it finally happen was still a shock.

He reached forward and clasped her hand. "I'm so sorry to leave London too."

She shook her head. "Don't be. You need to go there. We talked about it."

He sighed. "All the same. I do like to be where I'm needed. You see, Gerry has been finding some challenges with running the shop alone and I'd like to be there to help her. I assure you, I would not be going if I wasn't entirely sure that you were well situated."

She squeezed his hand. "I know. Gerry needs you right now. When are you leaving?"

"Sometime this week. Possibly as soon as tomorrow, if I can manage it. I didn't want to leave without seeing you first, but I think I have almost everything ready for my departure."

She tried to hide her surprise. "Are you buying a house, too?"

"Leasing one. At least for the moment. I may well settle there, but I prefer to see the place before making that decision, you know. I will send you a letter with my direction when I arrive so you can write to me."

"Thank you, Bertie."

"And darling," he went on. "If you ever need me urgently, come to my house and ask Thomas to let you into the workroom. He will understand. It might take me a few hours to get here, but I promise I will come immediately."

Nell wrapped her arms around Bertie's shoulders and gave him a hug, feeling a little tearful. "I'll miss you," she said.

"And I you, my sweet."

Bertie rang for tea while Charles described Gerry's shop in Tutting-on-Cress and life in the country. Then he left to give Bertie more time with Nell. Bertie prodded her with more questions about her new position, asking for details about the spells she was casting and what she was learning.

When they reached a lull in the conversation, he said,

"While you're here, darling, I wonder if I might solicit your help in tying up a loose end that has been troubling me."

"Of course," Nell said. "What is it?"

"Well, you see, I never did ask you why sweet Pip did not join you in your endeavor."

She was surprised by the question. "Oh, didn't I tell you? He didn't want to come."

"Ah," he said. "I do recall you saying that. He didn't happen to say why, did he?"

She shrugged. "I imagine he didn't want to leave Jack. You know they're together?"

Bertie pursed his lips. "Indeed," he said quietly. "I take it they have been together for quite some time."

"Almost since I left Jack the first time," she said. "And I did odd-jobs for years."

"I wonder," he said, "if we might provide him with the option."

Nell frowned. "He's had the option," she said. "I offered to bring him with me twice. He kept refusing it. I think he's more in love with Jack than he lets on. You should see the way they carry on," she added.

Bertie laughed. "I doubt my nerves could take it. Such pretty men, you know."

"Oh, they are always petting," Nell said. "Can't take their hands off each other. Jack, in particular."

"Couldn't take his hands off Pip?"

"Mm-hm."

"My, my. Such goings on," he said, his tone surprisingly mild. "I take it your friend Jack rather enjoys letting people see their...petting."

Nell laughed at the thought. "I rather think he does, yes. Used to make the rest of us pretty jealous, I can tell you. Such sounds Pip would make," she added with relish, hoping to see Bertie pretend shock.

To her surprise, he didn't. He merely looked thoughtful.

"Do you know," he said after a pause. "I've been thinking about what you've told me of the fellow. One to do little favors for people and collect debts, isn't he?"

"Yes," she said. "But he's very reasonable about it. I paid my debt with him twice. If you ask me, people take too big a cut when he pays them and that's why they get stuck."

"Is it possible that Pip has such a debt, do you think?"

"I suppose he might. He does have a mattress in our old room. But I imagine Jack gives him all that for free."

Bertie tilted his head in consideration. "I rather doubt your friend Jack gives anything away for free."

"You think that's why Pip stayed behind?"

"I think it's certainly possible."

She considered. "I never thought of that. It's not something I ever asked him."

"Of course, I could be mistaken, darling. Pip may choose to stay with him after all. But don't you think it would be better if he did so out of love rather than debt?"

"I suppose so. Mind you, I really don't think he's apt to leave Jack."

"Well, I confess I find myself frightfully curious. How do you fancy finding out?"

"You mean now?"

"Well, you know how I am, dear. So dreadfully flighty. I should like to resolve the situation before I leave town. Would you have time to go find out before you're due at the theater?"

Nell glanced at the clock. "I have a few hours before I'm due back."

"Excellent," he said. He walked her to his study and handed her a purse heavy with money as well as a pouch for a protection spell.

After Bertie helped her cast the spell, Nell took the money and left, reaching the tavern in record time. Jack was hunched over a pint when she walked in.

"Drinking already, Jack?" she asked jovially, excited to see his reaction.

He looked up at her, his eyes red-rimmed. "Nell," he said, getting up and pulling her into a bear hug. "Thank God you've come."

"Good Lord, Jack," she said, returning his hug with surprise. "It is good to see you, but I only came by to talk about Pip's debts. I was hoping I might be able to pay them off now that I'm better situated."

Jack pulled back, still keeping a tight grip on her arms. "You don't know then?"

"Know what?" she asked, feeling a sense of foreboding creep into her stomach.

He pulled her down to the bench.

"Jack," she said. "You're frightening me. Whatever is it?"

"Pip's been arrested," he said, his voice cracking. "He was caught pickpocketing yesterday afternoon and taken to Newgate."

Nell felt cold all over. "I have to go," she said hoarsely. "I have to see about getting him out. I'll find a way, Jack. I will."

She ran to Newgate Prison, with only the vaguest notion of a plan. There were, predictably, guards outside the prison doors. Just as predictably, none of them were the least bit interested in answering her questions about a pickpocket who was recently brought in. Most of them ignored her, a few sneered, and one got annoyed enough to threaten her with imprisonment for disturbing the peace. She hurried away after that, debating whether to go to Bertie for help or try another method.

An idea struck her like a flash, and she went with purpose to the market. She bought some rosemary, far more than she needed, in case her plan didn't work right away. Then she returned to the prison. She found a guard who was stationed far from the one who threatened her, palmed a sprig of rosemary, and sidled up to him.

"Excuse me, sir," she said in her sweetest voice as she cast the Motion spell for persuasion. "Could you give me some information about a friend of mine? He was arrested for pick-pocketing yesterday."

The guard gave her a sympathetic smile. "Against regulations, miss."

She discreetly cast the spell again. "I'd be much obliged if you made an exception. You see, my friend is...he's very sick. I need to see what I need to do to get him out and to a doctor."

The guard glanced around and then said quietly, "Oh, all right, ducks. You wait here and I'll find out. What's his name?"

"Standish. Philip Standish. Thanks ever so."

He gave her a wink and walked past the gate. She paced while she waited, fretting about whether the spell would still work when he was no longer in range. But a quarter of an hour later, he came back out. "Your friend hasn't been brought up to court yet," he told her. "But he's known to be a repeat offender. The judge he's getting isn't likely to go easy on him." He shrugged. "Not sure if you'll manage to get him out."

"Isn't there a bail or something I can pay?" Nell said.

He shook his head. "Sorry, ducks."

She gave the guard a nod of thanks and, with no other options left to her, she ran in a thoroughly undignified manner all the way back to Bertie's house.

She hurried into the study without waiting to be announced. "Pip's been arrested," she said, and burst into tears.

Bertie was at her side in a moment, pulling her to sit on the velvet settee. "It's all right, darling. It'll be all right. When did it happen?"

"Yesterday," she said, pulling out her handkerchief. "I've never seen Jack so upset. We can get him out, Bertie, can't we?

There must be a way. The guard said they won't let him out on bail and he's a repeat offender so the judge won't—but I thought perhaps you could—"

"Oh, darling, of course we will," Bertie said, covering her hands with his. "Charlie, dear, would you be so kind as to go to Tutting-on-Cress ahead of me?" She hadn't even realized Charles was back in the room.

"Of course, Bertie," Charles said.

"Good. And when you get there, please inform Gerry that I am bringing her a shop assistant."

Nell gasped. "Really, Bertie? You're taking him with you to the country? What if he doesn't want to—" She broke off. Of course Pip would opt to leave London if it meant getting out of prison. "I mean," she amended, "you're sure you can get him out?"

"Of course, darling, nothing to it. I'll have it all sorted out by the morning, I'm sure. Although I never did learn the sweet man's full name. Do you know it?"

"Philip Standish," she supplied.

"Excellent. Thank you, m'dear. Why, armed with that information, it'll be the simplest thing in the world. Pip and I will be in Tutting-on-Cress by dinnertime tomorrow night, I assure you. Would you like Charlie or myself to escort you back to the theater?"

She shook her head. "I'll be all right. You're sure you'll be able to get him out?"

"I am certain," he said. "And I will send you a note when I've secured his release. And another one when we're all settled in the country."

She gave him another hug. "Thank you, Bertie."

"I'm glad to do it, darling. I'll just talk to Charlie about getting the dear man some clothes and then we'll spring into action."

Nell gave Bertie his money back and left, barely paying attention to where she was going. That night, she did her work at the theater in a daze. She was thankful she had been on the same track for nearly a week. Betsy chided her a bit for not focusing.

When Nell explained her distress, Betsy said, "Not the quiet man who came to visit you?"

Nell nodded. "I've known him nearly all my life. I always used to keep him out of danger. I hate that I couldn't protect him from this."

Betsy put an arm around her shoulder. "He does seem to need protection, poor creature. Did you say your viscount friend promised to get him out?"

"Yes, Bertie seemed very confident."

Betsy squeezed Nell's shoulder. "Then I'm sure it will all work out. But it's no wonder you can't focus. Let's put you on a different track, though, so no one gets hurt. All right?"

Betsy pulled her to the easiest track for the rest of the night and Nell couldn't properly convey her gratitude for the gesture. She didn't relax until she received a note early the next morning from Bertie, assuring her that he had secured Pip's release and he would be taking Pip to the country immediately.

Nell cried in relief when she read the note. And then she cried again when she realized that nearly all of her friends, including Pip, had left her alone in London. Betsy and Harriet found her in her room. They sat on either side of her and pulled her into a tight hug.

"He's safe now," Betsy said. "That's what matters."

"But I may never see him again," Nell said. "I may not see any of them again. Now I don't have any more friends left in London."

"Well, I like that," Harriet said in a gently teasing tone. "What are we then? Yesterday's oatmeal?"

Nell gave a weepy laugh. "Sorry."

"She didn't want to presume," Betsy said in a mimicry of a posh accent.

Harriet blew a raspberry. "I like presumptions. Please presume that I am radiant and that I ought to make more money, and please presume that we are your friends."

"I'm not sure you understand the word," Betsy muttered.

Nell gave a less watery chuckle. "I'm glad you two are here."

Betsy pulled Nell's head to her shoulder, and Harriet leaned against her other side. She allowed their presence to comfort her. Perhaps she wasn't entirely alone after all.

CHAPTER 14

As the weeks went by, Nell found herself spending more and more time with Betsy and Harriet. She was pleased to discover that they were both from similarly humble backgrounds (although, admittedly, not quite as humble as her own) and had worked hard to get to where they were. She allowed herself to settle into her new life, gently letting go of her past and embracing her future. Gradually, she befriended more and more people at the theater and began to feel as if she had been accepted as a new member of the family.

She continued to keep in touch with all of her friends who now lived in the country. As promised, Bertie and Gerry both wrote to her regularly. Nell spent her free time writing replies back. She even included a letter to Pip in one of her letters to Bertie. She knew Pip couldn't read or write, but she decided it was safe to assume he was going to learn.

Once she was fully trained, Nell received one evening off each month, in addition to her biweekly day off. To her surprise, Harriet arranged for Nell's evening off to align with theirs and Betsy's.

"This way we can go out on the town together," Harriet explained. "You need a proper night out."

Nell suggested going to Jack's usual tavern and the others

agreed. After all, Nell now had a couple months' worth of pay. One evening, the three of them strode out of the theater together, Nell leading the way, Betsy and Harriet with their arms linked together behind her. Nell never had occasion to come into the courtyard in the evening before. She wasn't shocked by the sight of people soliciting wares or themselves, but it made her feel as if she had never left her previous haunts in the London streets.

"Where are you lot off to?"

She turned to see Lino leaning against a shop cart.

"Off to get a pint," she said. "It's our night off."

"Want to join?" Harriet asked.

He glanced around the courtyard, looking thoughtful. "It's always slow this time of year," he said. "All the wealthy folks run off to the country."

"You need to take some time off," Betsy added.

He turned back to look at them. Nell realized suddenly that he was anxious about the prospect of taking a night off. She wondered if he'd been struggling to find customers. He was very thin—was that his normal frame or the result of hard times? Her protective side took over.

"I'll buy you a pint," she said impulsively.

He grinned, and his expression made Nell also realize that Lino was very young. She wondered how much younger he was from her age. "Can't turn that down, can I?" he said. He pushed himself off the cart, looped his arm around hers in a mirror of the couple behind them. "Lead the way, Nelly."

Nell strode confidently through the streets of London and back down the alleyways she'd known her whole life, all the way to the tavern. She felt a pang upon entering it, knowing that Pip wouldn't be there. But Bertie had assured her that Pip was safe, and that was the most important thing. She wished too that Patience could have joined them. She felt sure Patience would like Betsy and Harriet. But Patience had made her feelings on such outings perfectly clear. There was no sense in wishing for the impossible. Besides, she had new friends now. It was time to move forward.

They found an empty table. Lino sat next to Nell on one side and Betsy and Harriet took the bench opposite. Nell ordered the group a round of pints, which made her feel wealthy and important. Just as they were all settling in to drink their ale, Nell felt a clap on her shoulder.

"Well, if it isn't Nell."

She turned and grinned up at Jack. "Good to see you, Jack. I brought some of my friends tonight. It's our night off."

"The rest of your drinks are on me," he said, which made Nell feel even more important. "Any friends of yours are welcome here any time."

Harriet raised their glass. "I like you already."

Jack laughed. "Pip told me you were working at the theater now. Are these friends from the theater?"

Nell nodded. "That's Betsy and Mx. Harriet," she said, pointing. "And this is Lino. He works...adjacent to the theater."

Lino shifted in his seat to look up at Jack over his shoulder.

Jack glanced down at Lino and then gave him a slow once-over. "Think I'll join you," he said, not taking his eyes off Lino.

Nell scooted to the side of the bench, expecting Jack to sit between her and Lino. Instead, he sat on Lino's other side, sitting in his usual way with his back to the table, which meant the two men were now easily facing each other.

Jack reached up and cupped Lino's chin. "Aren't you a lovely little thing?" he said in a low voice.

"Oh, yes," Lino said in a light tone. "It's the eyelashes, you know. Remarkably long."

Jack chuckled and swiped his thumb over Lino's cheek. "It's much more than that, sweet boy."

"I think we've lost him," Betsy remarked.

"Are you surprised?" Harriet said drily. "He *is* gorgeous."

Betsy snorted. "And he knows it."

"Well," Nell said. "It is his livelihood."

The three of them chatted while Jack continued to flirt with Lino. From what Nell could gather, Lino wasn't opposed. Jack placed a hand on Lino's thigh and Lino seemed to take it in stride. Although at one point, she heard Lino say in a slightly raised voice, "I'm afraid I'll have to start charging you for that."

She glanced over to see that Jack's hand had moved farther up Lino's leg. Lino looked unbothered by the touch and Jack seemed unbothered by Lino's tone. He said, "How much do you charge?"

Lino smirked. "Well, it depends on what you're wanting."

Jack grinned, reached into his pocket with his free hand, and pulled out a purse. To Nell's surprise, he dumped the contents of the purse onto the table. Then he leaned forward and murmured something in Lino's ear.

Lino began carefully sliding coins across the tabletop, his lips moving slightly as he counted the money. He paused at one point and said, "That much."

"And for you to stay the night?" Jack countered.

Lino counted out more coins.

Jack glanced at the amount. "You're undercharging, boy. You're worth more than that."

Lino shrugged. "It's my usual rate. Sometimes I charge more for certain customers and charge less for others."

"You should let me handle that part for you. We can charge double your rate. Even with my cut, you'd still make more."

Lino shook his head in a way that suggested they'd already had this exchange. "I work alone."

Jack kissed the corner of Lino's mouth. "We'll discuss it again in the morning. I plan to change your mind."

Lino's mouth quirked. "You'll find me very stubborn."

Then he separated the counted coins from the rest. "You want the night then?"

Jack nudged the remaining coins towards Lino. "Keep them." His smile turned sly. "I'm sure I can think of something else I want."

Lino shrugged and scooped the coins into his hand. Jack handed him the empty purse and stood. As Lino poured the coins into the purse and tucked it into his pocket, Jack slid a hand under Lino's open shirt and across his chest.

"I'm afraid we're going to leave you lot for the night," he said. He looked at Nell. "I'll make sure Bill knows to put all of your drinks on my account."

Harriet raised their glass. "Cheers."

Nell looked at Lino. "I guess you didn't get the night off after all."

He gave her an apologetic shrug. "Maybe next time."

Jack leaned down and kissed Lino's neck. "Come along."

Lino swung his legs over the bench and allowed himself to be guided through the tavern and up to Jack's room.

"I suppose I should have seen that coming," Betsy said.

"That Jack would take to Lino?" Nell said.

"That someone would take to Lino," Betsy replied.

"He was wrong, you know," Harriet said, taking a sip of ale. "It's not the eyelashes. It's those damn freckles."

The next night, Lino didn't show up at the theater and Nell guessed that Jack had had his way. She supposed Lino was now settling into Pip's former role. She could hardly fault Jack for moving on; Pip was unlikely to ever come back to London. Jack had needs, same as anyone else.

But the night after that, Nell was surprised to see Lino propped up on his usual stool by Archie's work space.

"What are you doing here?" she said without preamble.

He glanced over at her without moving his head. "Good to see you, too."

Archie huffed a laugh as he rouged Lino's cheeks.

"I thought you'd be with Jack."

Archie held up a small jar. "I think this would look wonderful on your lips."

Lino grinned. "You're the artist and I am but your humble canvas."

Archie chuckled and carefully rubbed coloring across Lino's lips. He held up a looking glass and Lino studied his reflection with evident pleasure. "Genius," he murmured. "Will it come off if I kiss you?"

"Yes," Archie said. "Save it for your customers."

Lino pouted. "And I thought you liked me."

Archie rolled his eyes and planted a kiss on Lino's cheek. "Off with you, you rascal."

Lino stood and looped his arm around Nell's. "In answer to your question," he said, leading her through the room. "He only hired me for the one night."

"But you weren't here last night."

He gave her a sidelong glance. "Yes, well, I barely had time to come back here and get a customer. I slept for most of today."

She gave him a more critical once-over. "You do look tired."

"Thanks," he said cheerfully.

"But why—" She broke off, unsure if it was actually appropriate to ask.

He led her to a corner of the room and then turned to look at her. "Why didn't I take him up on his offer?"

She nodded. "He takes care of his people."

He cocked an eyebrow. "Does he?"

"Yes. I never had to worry about whether I'd have enough to eat, or somewhere to sleep. I always knew I could fall back on him if I needed to. I left his employ because I wanted different work than what he could offer. But you—"

"Yes, I suppose I can see your confusion." He let out a long breath and leaned against the wall. "The way things are now, I get to choose which customers I go to bed with, which offers I accept. I get to choose how much they're going to pay me. We agree to terms. There are some customers I won't go home with and some I can only handle every now and again." He shrugged. "With someone like Jack taking charge, I wouldn't get any of that. He would decide who I went home with, how much my body and time is worth. He would determine the terms."

He gave her a careful look. "Let me put it this way: tonight, I can go out there and tell the first person who gives me a long glance that I can promise them an enjoyable time. If Jack were here, he would be on the lookout for those long glances and would be telling other people that I'm a treat in bed, and what I can do for them. Do you see?"

"I suppose," she said slowly. "Although I'm not sure I see the difference."

"Here's an example then: there's this customer. Sort of a regular. He likes to...he likes to give his partners pain. It's what he enjoys. It's just a taste, like anything else," he added, in response to her expression. "And some nights I don't mind it and I can take whatever he gives me. But the difference lies in my choosing to go home with him. I don't want anyone else deciding how much pain I can handle."

"I can certainly see that," Nell said.

He chuckled. "Don't fret. He pays me well, that one. But the thing is, I've never minded what I do. I'm good at it. I have a few regulars who I like quite a bit. I get to meet different people and figure out what they like. But if I were to have someone like Jack around, I would hate it. All of my choices would be taken away from me."

"That makes sense."

"I suspect that's why I like this work better than your friend Pip did."

Nell stared at him. "Pip wasn't a harlot."

Lino's eyes narrowed slightly. "Wasn't he?"

"No, of course not. He was just Jack's lover."

Lino opened his mouth and then closed it. He seemed to consider his next words for a moment. "Did you never wonder how we recognized each other?"

Nell blinked at him. "I...I did wonder," she said. "I just never worked it out."

Lino put a hand on Nell's arm. "Nelly," he said in a soft voice. "Jack used to take him here. He brought him most nights."

"He wouldn't!"

He gave her arm a gentle squeeze. "He did."

Nell opened her mouth to argue and then closed it as she thought back to how Pip had been in his last months in London. It also explained why Pip wasn't at the tavern when she'd visited at night, and why Jack was expected to return without him.

"Why didn't he tell me?" she said at last, annoyed by how hurt she sounded.

"Oh, love," Lino said, and pulled her against his chest. He rubbed her back. "He probably didn't know how," he said.

"But I always used to protect him. I would have—"

He pulled back to look at her. "You would have what? Hidden him away? Carted him off in the night?"

"I asked him to leave Jack and come with me but he never did," she said, knowing she sounded petulant and hating herself for it.

"Nelly," Lino said, his voice firm. "I've barely met Jack and I know plenty about him. You worked for him for years. Don't tell me you don't know that he has all of his people under his thumb. He traps them with debts and favors until they can't get free of them. They're stuck with him forever."

"How do you know about all that?"

"Everyone knows about that."

"Then why do people go to him?"

"Because they have nowhere else to go. If it's between

starving and being indebted to Jack Reid, many people choose debt. Although plenty of us would prefer to starve."

"You would?"

He raised his eyebrows. "I did."

"Oh." They were quiet for a long moment, and Nell thought back to how miserable and tired Pip had seemed, and how worse it had gotten before he was arrested. She felt a wave of guilt fill her.

"When Pip was arrested," Lino said, breaking into her thoughts, "who did you go to?"

"My friend, Bertie. Well, Lord Finlington."

"This Lord Finlington. He's a good sort of person? He won't take advantage of him?"

"He would never," she said. "I'm sure of it. Bertie is... Bertie's the best sort of person. He gives without expecting anything in return." Unlike Jack, she realized.

Lino smiled. "Then you did the right thing by him. You got him out, in the end. That's what matters." He squeezed her shoulders. "Don't waste your time on feeling guilty. It serves no purpose."

Nell thought about what Lino told her for weeks. She thought about it when Betsy assigned her to work on the special effects track, the most difficult one. She thought about it during her free time. She couldn't quite resist the feeling of guilt, despite Lino's advice.

One thing that somewhat assuaged her guilt was hearing from Gerry and Bertie, who stayed true to their promises to write. Even when their mentions of Pip were brief or vague, Nell was comforted in the knowledge that her friend was finally safe.

Bertie's letters detailed his new house in the country. He described it as "quaint" but it sounded almost as grand as the dukex's townhouse. He told her a little bit about his magical experiments, writing that he missed her assistance.

"I shall certainly need to think about hiring someone new," he

wrote. *"But I'm afraid I am frightfully picky about who I choose to work with. Not everyone is as easy to work with as you, my sweet."* He went on to say that he liked having an assistant who was eager to learn as well as to help. *"So perhaps I ought to focus my attention on acquiring a new pupil. I love teaching magic almost as much as I love studying it."*

When she wrote to him and asked how Pip was doing, he said he was doing well, but gave little details about Pip's new life. Gerry turned out to be a much better correspondent in that regard. She sent Nell thorough details of the house Charles had purchased and her new shop. She described her customers, her friends in the country, and how different it was from London.

"Pip is safely settled here," she assured her. *"He is frightfully good in the shop. All of the customers love him. I'm convinced he's the reason I'm selling half my stock at this point. No one can resist buying spells if it means the attractive and mysterious gentleman will be the one to sell them."*

Nell laughed at the idea of Pip turning on the charm he had honed as a pickpocket to use as a shop assistant.

"Unfortunately, he doesn't seem to feel entirely at home yet," Gerry admitted. *"Although I cannot determine if his melancholy is entirely circumstantial or if it is part of his character. In any case, we are all doing our best to help him. He's such a dear, sweet man. I can see why you care for him, and I can also see why you feel so protective of him. He has a gentle spirit that one wants to keep safe. Hopefully he will realize soon that he is part of our family now. Charles is very good at putting people at ease, so I'm confident it will turn out all right in the end."*

Nell was encouraged by her friend's letters. It worried her to learn that Pip was struggling to feel at home, but she knew if anyone could make a person feel welcome, it was Bertie, Gerry, and Charles.

So finally, after a full month of wrestling with her feelings on the matter, she decided to stop fretting about Pip. He was safe. He was protected, albeit by someone other than herself. She reminded herself that she already knew protecting Pip was no longer where she belonged and, as Lino had pointed out, she had managed to protect him one last time before he left London.

CHAPTER 15

NELL COULD ALMOST DESCRIBE her life as perfect now. She was fully trained at the theater and loved working there, she was surrounded by interesting people, most of whom came from similarly humble beginnings to herself, and she not only could do magic, but she was good at it. She was only missing one thing, and that missing thing was only really absent when she went to bed at night. As Betsy had warned her, she spent most of her nights with Harriet, so Nell had the little room to herself. She loved the privacy, but she missed the feeling of another body pressed up against her. She missed knowing touches, soft kisses, and tasting another person on her lips. After a couple months of thinking about it, Nell realized that she had a face to put to what she was missing. She missed Patience.

She was not, however, entirely sure whether Patience missed her. After their last conversation, she suspected that door was forever closed to her. But the more she thought about it, the more she realized she missed Patience as a friend as well as a bedmate. She missed the way the other woman would tell Nell when she was being too abrupt and the way she used to tease and flirt.

So, on her next full day off, Nell gathered her courage,

went to the market and bought a small loaf of sweet bread, and walked to Patience's house in the early evening. She was relieved when it was Patience who opened the door.

The other woman's eyes widened at the sight of her. "Didn't expect to see you again," she said.

"I know," Nell said.

Patience gave her a quick look up and down. "You look different...from the last time. Did something happen?"

"Yes, but it was something I wanted to have happen. May I come in?"

"The girls are up. I can't—"

"I just wanted to visit," Nell said. "We don't have to do anything. We can just talk." She held up the loaf. "I thought we could have some of this. Your little ones might like it."

Patience did not try to hide her surprise. But then, to Nell's relief, she smiled. "All right then. Come in."

Nell followed Patience into a tiny kitchen where they both sat at a table. Patience pulled her smallest child, Fanny, to her lap while Nell cut the bread. The older girl, Matty, took a slice and ran to eat it while she played. Patience fed Fanny bits of bread in between taking some bites for herself, and prompted Nell to tell her what had happened.

So Nell did. She wound up going as far back as the day she met Charles Kentworthy. She described the burglary, going to stay with Bertie, becoming friends with Gerry, and going to work at the theater.

After the whole story was over, Patience shooed Fanny away, brushed crumbs off her lap, and said, "Well, it seems like you've had quite an interesting few months."

"Some of it happened before. I mean, I told you about the time we met Bertie at the pub and everything. But yes. It's been very interesting."

Patience folded her hands on the table. "There's one thing I'm still trying to work out though."

"What is it?"

"Why did you come here today?" she said in a tone free of judgment or accusation. "I sent you packing months ago. I thought I'd never see you again." This last bit had been said in what Nell thought was a bit of a sad tone.

Nell shrugged. "I missed you, and I...I'd like to be friends again."

Patience was silent for a long moment. Finally she said, "I've missed you, too."

Nell felt as if she might faint with relief. "Oh, good."

Patience lifted an eyebrow.

"I thought you might send me packing again."

Patience gave her a small smile. "Well, if you keep on visiting me like this, we can see where it goes."

"Perfect," Nell said. She hesitated for a moment. "I don't get much time off from the theater."

"You say that like you think I'm going to suggest a holiday in Brighton or something. You think I have any time off to speak of?" Patience picked at the table. "But nothing's changed for me, you know. I'm still as boring and stuck at home as I was before."

Nell covered Patience's hand with her own. "I never said you were boring. I enjoy your company. I always have. I just...I just don't want what most people seem to want. What you were asking of me before...I don't think I can give it to you."

"What do you mean?"

Nell sighed. "I don't want to get married to anyone. I don't want to belong to anyone or have anyone belong to me. I'm not going to write any love letters and I have no interest in reading any either. I'm more apt to buy a loaf of bread for us to share than I am to buy you a posy for your kitchen table. Romance just isn't for me."

Patience rolled her eyes. "You idiot. You think I don't know that? I've known you ever since we were as young as my girls are now."

Nell gaped. "You don't mind then? It won't bother you if we want different things?"

"We've always wanted different things. I don't need to get married to be happy. I'm not interested in belonging to you and you've never belonged to anybody. Posies make me sneeze. The bread was much better than flowers anyway. I want this." She squeezed Nell's hand. "And maybe a bit of what we had before. But better."

"You'd be happy with just...just friendship?"

"I'd hardly describe friendship as 'just' anything, Nelly."

Nell leaned forward and kissed Patience's cheek. "Thank you."

Patience smiled. Then her smile turned a bit intrigued. "Did you say something about writing love letters?"

Nell groaned. "Please don't tell me you want them."

"No..." Patience said in a musing tone. "But I wouldn't mind learning how to read. We could trade for it. You teach me and I'll do that thing you like with—"

Nell held up a hand. "Absolutely not."

Patience pouted.

"I'll teach you to read because we're friends. But I've never taught anyone. So I'm not sure how good I'll be."

Patience's smile was wide. "I don't mind. You'll really teach me?"

"Course. We can even teach your little ones when they're old enough. Then they won't have to depend on Jack's charity."

Patience reached up, cupped the back of Nell's neck, and pulled her in for a kiss. "I'm so glad you came back, Nelly."

Nell walked from her friend's door back to the theater, ruminating how one good deed—saving Charles from thieves —had turned out to have such a huge impact on her life. It was strange to think how that one fateful day had been mere months ago. Now here she was, living a life she used to dream about. She had spent so long trying to find her place in the world. It hadn't been in Jack's tavern, or Smelting's spell shop, or in Bertie's study.

As she walked through the London streets, she realized that she hadn't found her place after all; she had carved it out with her own two hands.

The End

NOTE FROM THE AUTHOR

Dear Reader,

I hope you enjoyed Nell's journey.

My aim with all of my books is to give queer characters the opportunity for joy. I wanted to tell a story with an aromantic character who is still proudly aro at the end of the novel and who doesn't have to compromise who she is in order to find happiness.

Jane Austen once wrote, "There are as many forms of love as there are moments in time." This book was an important cornerstone in my series that seeks to depict love and queer joy in their many beautiful forms.

Affectionately,

Sarah Wallace

ACKNOWLEDGMENTS

Once again, this book wouldn't exist without my amazing support network. To Ashley, the first person to read this story, thank you for encouraging me throughout this whole process, and for helping me to polish it in its final state. To Alexis, thank you for the green highlights that tell me when I'm doing something right. Thank you to Emily, who helped me brainstorm a good conflict when I was feeling stuck. Thank you to Kayla, who was the first person to recommend splitting the original draft into two separate stories. To my beta readers: Katie, Karen, and Allison, thank you for providing me such valuable feedback. You helped me to shape my story and gave me some much needed confidence! Thank you to my incredible editor, Mackenzie Walton, who, as always, helps me bring my stories up several notches (and for telling me I'm strong at revision. I would like that on my tombstone, please). And thank you to Salt & Sage for providing a sensitivity read of my first aromantic character.

Editor: Mackenzie Walton
Proofreader: Ashley Scout
Historical Consultant: Alexis Howard
Sensitivity Reader: Salt & Sage Books
Front cover photo by Giusi Borrasi via Unsplash
Back cover photo by Sonder Quest via Unsplash
Author photos by Toni Tillman

ABOUT THE AUTHOR

Sarah Wallace lives in Florida with her cat, more books than she has time to read, a large collection of classic movies, and a windowsill full of plants that are surviving against all odds. She only reads books that end happily.

ALSO BY SARAH WALLACE

Letters to Half Moon Street

The Glamour Spell of Rose Talbot - free to newsletter subscribers!

Next in Meddle & Mend

The

Education

of

Pip

Coming in 2023

PREVIEW FOR LETTERS TO HALF MOON STREET

From Geraldine Hartford
   Shulfield Hall, Tutting-on-Cress
To Gavin Hartford
   8 Half Moon Street, London

28 August 1815

Dear Gavin,

Mama has written to me about her scheme to send you to London. I thought having a letter waiting for you when you arrive might be a pleasant surprise. You will likely be a grump about the whole thing for you do not enjoy having your life upset, but surely you will not want to be at home when John and Veronica take over the house. You and John have never gotten along in the best of circumstances. Living together while his wife goes through her confinement will only exacerbate things. Goodness knows what sort of chaos will ensue when her baby is actually born. Mama is quite right to send you away. You know I do not say that lightly.

Before you ask, no, I will not come and help you settle in London. I am having a capital time with our cousins and have no interest in leaving.

I believe living alone in town will do you some good. You want a little independence, my dear brother. Please do not spend all of your time in the library.

And do try to enjoy yourself.

Affectionately,

Gerry

FROM GAVIN HARTFORD
   8 Half Moon Street, London
TO GERALDINE HARTFORD
   Shulfield Hall, Tutting-on-Cress

1 September 1815

GERRY,

London is already a right bore. If you were a kind sister, like you ought to be, you would not make me suffer alone. Terribly unsporting of you.

Mother was in a fine state before I left. She had the servants going through all the usual household spells, making sure every part of the house was spotless. I don't see why she bothers. Veronica is happiest when she feels superior, so a less than perfect house will make her more eager than ever to be mistress of it someday.

When Mother first suggested this scheme, I thought she was sending me to London only to get me out of the house temporarily. But it seems she intends for me to stay until after the baby is born. She even said I might as well stay for six months or more. She has insisted I will be in the way. It is absurd for her to be in such a state. Veronica is unlikely to actually take Mother's advice on anything, and will only frustrate everybody.

Oh, and Father sat me down and went over all of the business he wants me to take care of while I am in London. I suppose I should be grateful he did not foist these responsibilities upon me sooner. And I daresay I'm glad I'm not the firstborn. Having that much responsibility would be even worse, even with the benefit of inheritance. At any rate, Father said the real reason I am staying here is to see to it that the townhouse is prepared for the Season, and he gave me a list of things he wants taken care of. He also said if I do well enough at all of this, I might be able to continue with it as an actual career—acting as steward on John's behalf. I shudder to imagine it. I really must find an occupation for myself, and soon. I did notice Father did not alter the timeline Mother put forth. So I suspect this list of responsibilities is merely to keep me busy. What a great bother it all is.

Our townhouse in London was outrageously warm when I arrived. I'm glad I wasn't sent here at the height of the summer. As it was, I had to dash around the house to help the servants open the windows. Then I had to set up at least a dozen cooling spells. Cook already needs more mint for the purpose. I still have that tendency to overload my spells with too much magical power, so the cooling spells ought to have made the place frigid. And yet, it is still too warm. It would be far better if you were here to help me.

I confess I am thoroughly intimidated by the city. Father gave me directions to the club we're members of. I had initially planned to walk there. I'm accustomed to walking or riding everywhere back at home, but I am far too nervous about getting lost. I took a hackney the first time I went to Nesbit's Club, and I was immediately confused by all the turns and the traffic. I am sure you will scold me, but I cannot countenance going anywhere other than the club at this juncture.

Did you go to Nesbit's when you were in town? I own I did not know what to expect. I liked the quiet atmosphere, but I was alarmed by the number of people inside. I went straight to the dining room and found a little table in the corner. I sat next to a lovely stained glass window, which was pleasant, and no one approached me, which was a relief. It was unsettling, though, to sit in a dining room amongst strangers and to be completely alone.

Now I am alone in London and it may be months before I can leave. Until the Season begins in earnest, there is precious little to do. Not that I would relish being here when the Season is at its peak, for you know I do not enjoy suffering through so much society. Even with Father's list of responsibilities, I am not exactly busy. I daresay I'm grateful for that, but I feel sure I shall forget something. Practically all I have to occupy my time is to dine at Nesbit's Club, which is hardly diverting. At home, I could hide in books all day, but the library in our London house is nothing to the library at home. It would serve our parents right if I gambled away my funds out of sheer boredom.

Give my regards to our cousins.

Affectionately,

Gavin

From Geraldine Hartford
Shulfield Hall, Tutting-on-Cress
To Gavin Hartford
8 Half Moon Street, London

4 September 1815

Dear Gavin,

You know Mama. Once she has a scheme in her head she must have her way.

Do you remember when our cousin said Tutting-on-Cress was simply filled with eligible bachelors? Now that I am here, I am convinced Rose was fibbing. There are precious few single men around. Besides, I'm fairly sure Rose fancies another woman in the village. So I have no idea why she was even considering gentlemen suitors. From what Aunt Lily has said, there was some sort of to-do in the spring—something about a dashing bachelor. Rose has been tight-lipped on the details, but I suppose it's possible for her to be of the feminine persuasion and still have her head turned by a particularly handsome man. If I learn more, I shall tell you.

In any case, attempting to win a husband is an exhausting

experience. So I'm not opposed to simply enjoying my time here, rather than continuing the search. I have not admitted any of this to Mama yet. I think she will be disappointed about the lack of prospective suitors, but I doubt she will mind me staying here indefinitely. She trusts me to behave well around John even less than she trusts you. You will simply grumble and lock yourself up in the library. But suffering under John's company, I might actually put a curse on him, brother or no.

You cannot convince me there is nothing for you to do. Is there no one you can talk to at our club? You do know Nesbit's caters to the intellectual set, don't you? I'm sure you could find someone there who shares an interest in poetry or magic or something. Of course, you would have to actually talk to them to discover this. I certainly hope you do not intend to spend your entire time in London without talking to anybody.

I agree with you on the subject of the library in the town-house. Try Hatchard's Bookshop. They kept me quite afloat while I was in London.

I don't believe you would be such a pinhead as to gamble away your money. But I think it might do you some good to be reckless, so I will not talk you out of it. I warn you, however, that I shall not lend you my money. The shops in Tutting-on-Cress are excellent, despite it being a small town, and there are plenty of things I wish to buy.

Affectionately,
Gerry

FROM GAVIN HARTFORD
   8 Half Moon Street, London
TO GERALDINE HARTFORD
   Shulfield Hall, Tutting-on-Cress

7 September 1815

GERRY,

You may not believe it, but I have already completed Father's list. Well, some of the items must be repeated throughout my stay, but I have managed to take care of everything else. I suppose Father may be right about this being a suitable career for me. I mean to say, I did not find anything he had me do at all difficult. I might even consider it as a viable option, but I truly cannot countenance having to answer to John for the rest of my life. I have a suspicion Father knows this and is looking to oust me from my current state of indecision.

I am sure I would not mind finding a career for myself, but I haven't the faintest idea of what I should do. I am not clever enough for law, nor to be a professor. I'm sure I haven't the stomach to be a doctor, nor the proper gravity to be a vicar. And I know what you shall say: I have more than enough gravity. You take my meaning. I have not the soul of a vicar. Besides, vicars have to talk a great deal to people quite regularly and I'm sure I should hate that. Come to think of it, law poses the same problem. So does the medical profession. And teaching. Blast it. I wish I could be like you and Seb and simply look for a spouse. But the very notion of such a task fills me with utter dread. I want to retch just thinking about it.

My evenings at the club have been very strange lately. The manager keeps asking me if I would like to be introduced to people. Did she ever do that to you? I told her I knew no one in London, and then she said apparently some people would like to know me. This was a terrifying prospect, so I begged her to discourage them as politely as she could. She gave me an odd look but did as I asked. I have taken to practically inhaling my food in order to prevent this from happening again. I would take my meals at home but it is far too hot for such a thing.

If you were here, we could make a merry party of it at the club together. I'm sure you will tell me you have acquaintances in town and you would be perfectly happy to meet new people. Even if I were forced to suffer through some amount of society, it would be far less horrifying if I had someone to do it all with me.

Is there no chance I can persuade you to come stay in London?

Affectionately,
Gavin

READ THE REST OF LETTERS TO HALF MOON STREET, *AVAILABLE* *at all retailers.*

SIGN UP FOR THE NEWSLETTER!

ARE you signed up for my newsletter? Join now at sarahwallacewriter.com to be in the know!

NEWSLETTER SUBSCRIBERS ARE THE FIRST TO SEE BOOK COVERS, receive the first chapter of new releases a month before release date, get sneak peeks at preorder campaign art, and a free novelette! I've also been known to send deleted scenes or scenes in alternate POV and I plan to do more of that!

Read on for a preview of the free novelette *The Glamour Spell of Rose Talbot*.

PREVIEW FOR THE GLAMOUR
SPELL OF ROSE TALBOT

THE WHOLE AFFAIR began when Mr. Harry Bowden abandoned all apparent sense and fell in love with Miss Kitty Corley.

"It is the outside of enough," Rose Talbot groused to her friend, Julia Hearst. "Everyone knows that I have set my cap at Mr. Bowden. And everyone knows Miss Corley is the prettiest girl in Tutting-on-Cress. Why must she have everything?"

Julia Hearst took a bite of shortbread and did not reply. The two ladies were sitting in the drawing room, having tea. When Mr. Hearst had died two years ago, he had left his young wife in possession of a small cottage and a modest income. Julia was a sensible woman, sensible enough to manage on said modest income and sensible enough not to intervene when Rose was in a *mood*.

"I truly do not understand what everyone finds so special about Miss Corley," Rose continued. "Yes, she is utterly beautiful. Yes, she has the most perfectly golden hair with those perfectly tiny curls that frame her face just so. Yes, her eyes are very blue and her figure is very trim. And yes, she plays the pianoforte better than I do and has the voice of a veritable angel." Rose paused, having lost track of her argument. "Oh, bother," she said. "She's utterly perfect, of course. But, must she be all that *and* have secured Mr. Bowden's affections? It hardly seems fair."

Julia set her cup down and looked at her friend.

Rose had rather hoped that Julia would agree with her. Better yet, she'd hoped Julia would point out some of Miss Corley's faults. It would have made her feel far better about her circumstances if Julia would simply tell her that she was far superior to the new object of Mr. Bowden's affections. Unfortunately, Julia was simply looking patient and sympathetic, which was not nearly as satisfying.

"I know you are not fond of him," Rose said, finally giving up on expecting Julia to say what she wanted to hear. "But I do believe Mr. Bowden to be quite the most perfect gentleman of my acquaintance. He is clever, dark and mysterious, and he has a lovely smile. And I'm sure no one else has paid me the same attention that he has." She sighed. "What shall I do?"

"Perhaps," Julia said at last, "he is not worth your time, my dear, if he is so easily swayed. After all, to all appearances, he seemed about to propose to you only last month."

"Exactly!" Rose said, pointing with her biscuit for emphasis, a lapse in manners she would only dare in Julia's safe company. "I, for one, should like to know how she managed it."

"Then again," Julia continued quietly, "I seem to recall everyone being completely certain he would propose to Miss Worcester only last Season."

"Well, Lizzy Worcester's a bit of a ninnyhammer. I can't say I'm surprised by that turn of events. He probably just got her started on the right topic. You know how she gets."

"I rather like Lizzy," Julia said in a mild tone.

Rose opened her mouth to reply and then closed it. "Yes, I suppose she's all right," she said at last.

"I have always found it odd," Julia said, "that his interests invariably lay with the wealthiest ladies in the county."

"Oh, well, that is unfair," Rose said. "Is he not to inherit his father's fortune and title? I cannot believe him to be a fortune hunter. I am sure you are wrong."

"But three such different girls in the span of a year?" Julia persisted. "It is not normal."

"I seem to recall Lady Windham courting several young ladies in quick succession in much the same manner. Including your Miss Worcester," Rose said in a smug tone.

Julia sipped her tea. "Very true, my dear. But Caro Windham is hardly a good example. She has been married to Maria for over a year and is still one of the most brazen flirts I have ever encountered. Mr. Bowden may not be a fortune hunter, but he may well be another Lady Windham, in his way."

Rose frowned at this observation. "I do not think that is likely. I just wish things were as they once were."

Julia gave her friend a sympathetic smile and patted her knee. "Well, I am sorry, dear. I know how fond of him you were."

Rose heaved a sigh of the deeply aggrieved. "I still am, Julia. That is the untoward tragedy of it all."

Rose left her friend's cottage, her mind still filled with thoughts of the dashing Mr. Bowden. She thought of his dark brown hair, with the curl that fell over his forehead in that charming way. She thought of his lovely dark eyes that seemed to hook her in with a glance so that she couldn't look away. She thought of his mouth and all of the wonderfully intelligent things that came out of it. She sighed, feeling mournful. Truthfully, she never did entirely follow all of the intelligent things that Mr. Bowden said. But it was lovely to hear him say them. Was that why he had thrown her over for the far-too-perfect Miss Corley?

She wondered to herself how Miss Corley got to be so disgustingly perfect. Everyone in town was practically in love with Miss Corley. Rose continued to ponder, shamelessly enjoying the self-pity. It stood to reason that Mr. Bowden would inevitably fall under her spell.

Rose stopped. Perhaps that was it! It would explain everything. Perhaps Mr. Bowden had fallen under Miss Corley's *spell*. It was possible that the entire town had fallen under it. She wondered, a bit fretfully, if she had fallen under it too, and grimaced at her recent begrudging praise of the woman.

She put a hand to her cheek. Poor Mr. Bowden! He had fallen in love against his will. She clenched her fist. There was nothing for it. She had to fight back. She had to fight for Mr. Bowden.

READ THE REST OF THE GLAMOUR SPELL OF ROSE TALBOT *by subscribing to Sarah Wallace's newsletter at sarahwallacewriter.com.*

9 781737 432715